MW01059002

JACK TEMPLAR and the LORD OF THE WEREWOLVES

Book #4

A NOVEL

Jeff Gunhus

JACK TEMPLAR
and the
LORD OF THE WEREWOLVES

Printed in the United States of America

Cover design by Eric Gunhus
Cover Art by Nicole Cardiff
Edited by Sher A Hart
Formatting by Rik Hall

Library of Congress Cataloging-in-Publication Data
Gunhus, Jeff
Jack Templar and the Lord of the Werewolves: a novel / Jeff Gunhus
ISBN-13: 978-0-9899461-5-5
ISBN-10: 0-9899461-5-0

ALSO BY JEFF GUNHUS

MG/YA FICTION

Jack Templar Monster Hunter
Jack Templar and the Monster Hunter Academy
Jack Templar and the Lord of the Vampires
Jack Templar and the Lord of the Werewolves

ADULT FICTION

Night Chill
Night Terror
Killer Within

NON-FICTION

Reaching Your Reluctant Reader
Wake Up Call
No Parachute Required
Choose The Right Career
The Little Book Of Secrets

Praise for Jack Templar Monster Hunter
The Templar Chronicles Book 1

Selected as a 2012 Finalist for the Book of the Year Award. – *Foreword Reviews*

Selected as a Parent's Choice Foundation Recommended Read and as a Finalist for Next Generation Indie Book Awards

"Gunhus brings young readers a monster-filled romp to read at their own risk. The pacing is quick but not rushed, and events seamlessly progress, complete with action, cliffhangers and surprise reveals. " - *Kirkus Reviews*

"The action starts right from the first chapter and doesn't let up until the book ends. This is the first book in a series, and I look forward to reading the rest of them." -*The DMS*

"Jeff Gunhus has made a terrific fast paced fantasy. I even wanted to bolt my doors and lock my windows! Five stars for the best book of the year." - *Elizabeth A. Bolt*

"Move over Harry Potter and Percy Jackson, there's a new kid in town - Jack Templar, and he will take you on a wonderful adventure of good vs evil, with friends and enemies at every turn." -*Penny Brien*

Praise for Jack Templar and the Monster Hunter Academy
The Templar Chronicles Book 2

"Jeff Gunhus has crafted another winner in the sequel to Jack Templar: Monster Hunter…in another captivating story filled with plot twists and turns." - *Mother Daughter Book Reviews*

"This book is spellbinding…Please hurry and finish the rest of the series." – *Charlotte Edwards*

"I would highly recommend these books to anyone who loves adventure and fantasy. Riordan fans will definitely love this series! It's exactly what a middle grade fantasy should be." – *N. Hewitt*

"Holy cow, this book was amazing, just amazing! I don't even know what else to say other than to fangirl all over the place…You have to read this book. Just ... read it." – *K. Sozaeva*

"The characters leap off the page and grab the reader and draw him or her into the always dangerous, sometimes deadly adventures. This is a series that demands to be read." – *Michelle S. Willms*

"I think anyone who loves an action packed children's book should read this one. You won't be disappointed." – Christina Condy

Praise for Jack Templar and the Lord of the Vampires
The Templar Chronicles Book 3

"Mr. Gunhus has once again created a story that his young readers will have trouble putting down until the last word is read and wanting to follow Jack's next adventure in Book Four." – *Christina Weigand*

"This is the third book of the series, and I fear I must now declare myself addicted. I rapidly read this book and was depressed when I realized I now have to wait for the next book." – *J. Rivera*

"The adventures that Jack Templar goes through are awesome. This series is a great read for middle-grade children and young adults." – *Dalene's Book Review*

"Continuing with an exciting story. Loved the twists and turns in this book." – *Cheryl Carpinello*

"Hands down the THE BEST book out there! My boys were begging to stay up later to find out what the next chapter would reveal." – *Heidi Silvestri*

For my own little monsters:

Jackson, William, Daniel, Caroline and Owen

And for Nicole: who always smiles when
she tells me to go write.

My name is Jack Templar.

Just before my fourteenth birthday, I discovered that I came from a long line of monster hunters. You know, vampires, werewolves, zombies, all kinds of evil creatures called *Creach*.

Not only that, but if monsters around the world could choose one human to kill, it would be me. Why? I used to say I didn't have a clue, but that's not true. Not anymore.

As the last Templar Knight, I'm on a quest to reunite the five mystical Jerusalem Stones so that I can defeat Ren Lucre, the Lord of the Creach who holds my father hostage and threatens to launch a war against the human world. I managed to get the first Jerusalem Stone from the Lord of the Vampires after a battle under the streets of Paris. One down, four to go.

Only a few months ago, I was just a kid worrying about school. Now I'm a monster hunter with the fate of the world on my shoulders.

It's been quite a ride.

WARNING

If you're reading this, there's a good chance you've read my first three books. In that case, you've already ignored my previous warnings and decided to join the fight against the Creach. Thank you.

But on the off chance you stumbled across this book at your friend's house or it was given to you by someone who didn't understand the implications of possessing this book, there are a few things you need to know.

First, monsters are real. Vampires, werewolves, zombies, demons, you name it. In fact, they are more common than you could ever imagine. Second, this book is not make-believe. This is a truthful account of my life as a monster hunter and the dangerous mysteries that often surround me. Third, reading this book makes you fair game for monsters.

That last one is very important. If you read this book, you become both a hunter and the hunted. You'll need to be ready to face the monsters in your area because they will come looking for you. Take some time before turning the page to make sure you're up to the challenge. There's no turning back.

Whether you have been with me from the beginning or are new to the fight, be warned that my adventures are getting more serious. The forces of darkness are gathering and this book doesn't pull any punches. But I owe it to you to tell you the truth. Even if it's scary. Even if it's sad.

So turn the page if you dare. The adventure starts now.

Jack Templar

P.S. Go to www.JackTemplar.com for hunting advice and to see photos of some of the places I visit in this adventure. Use the password MONSTER to enter the secret Hunters Only area for extra treats. See you there.

Prologue

The stench hung heavy in the air. There was no other smell in the world quite like it. First came the stink of grease fires from the wall torches, the heavy black smoke that roiled through the air like a foul fog. Then a moldering, musty base layer came to the senses. It reeked of decay and seeping moisture that grew black mold on every surface. The mold clung on the rough-cut rocks lining the dungeon tunnels. It covered the thick iron bars holding the prisoners in place. It even grew on the tattered rags covering the miserable creatures in the cells and likely on their skin as well. That final smell overlay the symphony of stink.

The Creach prisoners.

Werewolves, harpies, blind mad-worms, blinderwursts, fangpiercers, even some demons held with the special pure iron chains required to keep them in place. Many of these creatures were pungent under the best circumstances, but locked in the deepest dungeon underground, sometimes for decades, they took on an odor so ripe, so awful, that visitors to the dungeon often had to hold their breath to enter. Even then, the smell would make their eyes sting and well with tears.

Immediately after leaving the dungeon, visitors were allowed a bath or a shower in the castle. As they washed the stench from their bodies, they would feel an overwhelming sense of thanks that they were not a prisoner wallowing in the horrifying conditions they'd just witnessed.

No one, human or Creach, wanted to be a prisoner in the dungeons of Ren Lucre.

Far away, at the end of one of the long, twisting corridors, came the creak of a massive door opening. The prisoners stirred at the sound. Their reactions mirrored how long they had been in their cells.

The newer arrivals looked up with expectation, still hopeful their punishment was going to be short and that someone was coming to tell them their nightmare was over.

Those who had been there longer knew that hope was useless in this dark place. They simply cowered farther into whatever dark corner they could find in their cell, desperate not to be noticed by the Master.

Then there were those who had been there the longest. They simply looked up with mild interest, knowing that nothing they did made any difference. Their spirits were broken. Worse, they knew this to be the dark truth, and they simply didn't care.

One single prisoner reacted in none of these ways. He simply stood, and the rags that had once been his clothes hung on his bony frame. Unbroken by years of starvation and torture, he still squared his shoulders in the direction of the sound and raised his chin, his eyes glistening in the torchlight with defiance. What he saw would have brought a normal man to his knees, but this man was no more normal than the monster approaching.

Ren Lucre, the five hundred year old vampire, filled the hallway as he strode through it, his cloak billowing behind him as he rushed past the stinking cells. His pale, narrow face looked pinched and concerned. His blood-red lip pursed in a straight line, and his eyes glowered like embers in a fire that might at any time combust into new flame.

He came to the thick set of bars that held the proud man, stopped, and stared him down.

"Well, if it isn't the Lord of the Creach," the man said. Even though his voice was course and weak, he still managed an edge of bitter sarcasm. "You look like you're having a bad day." The man spat on the floor. "Good."

Ren Lucre shook his head and looked away,

making a decision. "Do you know why I don't kill you?" he finally asked.

"I figured it was because you enjoyed my company," the man replied.

An ogre in the cell next to the man howled in amusement. Ren Lucre glared at him, a hand going to the sword at his waist. The ogre licked his lips expectantly as if seeing death as a welcome relief from the dungeon. But Ren Lucre turned away, not giving the creature any release from this world.

The man pointed to the ogre with a thumb. "Ognard here gets me."

Ren Lucre smiled, but the hatred in the expression was clear. "Good, maybe you and Ognard should share a cell."

The man stopped smiling. "One of us would end up dead. It wouldn't be me, but it wouldn't be pretty."

Ren Lucre sneered. "It's enough to see your infernal smirk gone. The reason I haven't killed you is so I can make you suffer. And I think I've done a pretty good job of that, don't you?"

"I only suffer when you come down here and stink up the place. It takes weeks for your odor to clear out of here once you leave." He looked around to the Creach in the cells around him. "We all talk about it behind your back, don't we, guys?"

The other Creach hissed and growled at the man, but they cast worried looks at Ren Lucre as well.

The vampire simply smiled. "I've struggled to decide how much I should tell you about what's happening in the world. Not sure if the news I have will give you hope or despair."

"Try me," the man said.

"How long do you think you've been in here?" Ren Lucre asked.

"Hard to say, time flies when you're having this much fun. I'd say about –"

"Fourteen years," Ren Lucre said. "Just over actually."

For the first time, a flash of concern passed over the man's face. "Impossible," he whispered.

"I'm afraid not," Ren Lucre said. "As you said, time flies."

"Fourteen years," the man mumbled, making the connection. He looked up suddenly, not saying the name filling him with dread.

Ren Lucre smiled, showing his long canines.

"Oh yes, Jack. I went to visit him myself on his fourteenth birthday." He paused, enjoying the fear on the man's face. "But he escaped."

The man let out a sigh of relief. "So... he's still alive?"

Ren Lucre nodded. "Yes, the little fool sought out and found my daughter, the Lord of the Vampires. Somehow convinced her to give him one of the Jerusalem Stones from what my spies tell me. Father-to-father, I can share with you that this little indiscretion really disappointed me."

"Why does Jack want the Jerusalem Stone?" the man asked as much to himself as to Ren Lucre.

"My guess is that he's going after the others next to reunite the Stones like the legends say."

"No," the man said, slumping to the ground on

his knees, head hung low. "Oh, Jack, no."

"Ahhh..." Ren Lucre said, smiling broadly. "That's it. That's the moment I wanted to see." He leaned forward and poked a finger in the man's direction. "That very second when you fully understood that you and your kind will be completely defeated... and that your own son will be the one who brings it upon you." He closed his eyes as if savoring the taste of his favorite meal. "Thank you for that. That's all I needed. Thank you."

Ren Lucre spun around and stomped back the way he had come, leaving the man kneeling on the floor.

John Templar shook his head and, for the first time in his life, hoped desperately for his son to fail.

Chapter One

It seemed impossible to digest that Ren Lucre, the Lord of the Creach, the one raising an army to destroy the world, the monster who most wanted me dead and who kept my father prisoner in his dungeon, was actually my grandfather.

But I knew my friends deserved the truth, so on the first day on the boat leaving Paris, I told them everything. They were shocked, of course, and didn't know what to say.

Will, my scrappy friend from Sunnyvale, put an

arm around me. He'd stuck by my side during my whole crazy adventure into the world of Creach, monster hunters, and ancient prophecies. "Wow," he said. "And I thought my family was messed up."

It was the perfect comment. Five out of six of us laughed, including T-Rex, my other friend from middle school, along with Xavier and Daniel, who I'd met at the Monster Hunter Academy. Then we spoke openly about what my monster relatives meant to our mission – stopping Ren Lucre from destroying human civilization – and how each of us felt about it. Not that it solved anything, but it did make sure we all had the same information. Everyone felt better afterward, everyone except the sixth member of our party who stood silently staring out into the night. It was an unspoken understanding that the best way to handle that situation was to just give it time and leave it alone. She would come around eventually. We hoped.

But that was three days ago and, with night closed in around us, the stress of our situation made the companionship of that moment seem far away.

I turned my back on my friends and stared up at the moonless night sky. I felt the gentle movement on the river as it carried our boat west, away from Paris. The bank slid by silently on my right, just a dark shadow of trees.

"I can't take any more of this endless debate," Daniel said behind me. "I say we fight, and the winner chooses our next move."

I clenched my hands into fists and wondered whether I should just let them give Daniel my answer. I turned to gauge whether the comment had been a joke to release the tension or a real suggestion. Neither would have surprised me.

Daniel stepped toward me and, by the look on his face, I don't think he was sure either whether he'd been joking or not. He was taller than me by a foot and built like a star high school quarterback, with broad shoulders and thick twists of lean muscle. His once ridiculously good looks now had the blemish of a fake nose attached to his face where a swarm had screechers had chewed off the original. Even though I'd saved him from dying that day and we've been friends and fought side-by-side ever since, some of the old tensions between us still leaked out every now and then.

He and I hadn't exactly gotten off on the right foot when I'd arrived as the new guy at the Monster Hunter Academy. The ancient school in France served as the training grounds for the Black Guard, the secret society tasked with protecting the reg, or regular, world from the Creach. He was already top dog there when I showed up with everyone whispering about the prophecy, about how I might be "the One," how I was the last Templar knight. There's nothing a top dog like Daniel appreciates less than another dog showing up and peeing in his yard. Well, peeing in his front yard and then trying to steal his ex-girlfriend is worse. Yeah, that happened too. Worst of all, he still had a thing for her.

All that was supposed to be behind us now. We were friends, comrades-in-arms who'd faced down screechers, dragons, goblins, desert djinn and even an entire vampire horde together. Still, under the stress of the last few days, we were at each other's throats.

"Back down, you idiots," said a voice from behind us. It was Will. "You guys are acting like morons. You're just tired. We all are."

He stepped between us like the mini-pit-bull he was, pushing each of us back with a hand. Because of his small size, enemies often underestimated Will, and sometimes his friends did too. But I knew no one tougher or more loyal. Out of respect for him, and because neither of us really wanted to fight, Daniel and I backed away from one another.

Will was dressed in the same gear we all had, black pants, black t-shirt, and a jacket with multiple pockets. Exactly the same outfits we'd all been wearing three days earlier when we battled the vampire horde in the catacombs of Paris.

Three days ago.

It seemed like a lifetime.

Especially since that was how long it had been since any of us had more than an hour or two of fitful sleep.

"That's better," Will said. "We're all tired and more than a little grumpy, so let's just assume people are going to say dumb stuff they don't mean, okay?"

"Like when I said I wasn't hungry," said another voice. "I was just kidding about that."

T-Rex, piped up from the opposite side of the small steering house in the center of the boat. He stepped out, hand on his oversized stomach, looking unhappy. I smiled at him not because of what he said but because his presence on this adventure always reminded me about the strength of friendship. He was here because he would do anything to help his friends. And if that meant traveling halfway around the world to battle monsters, so be it. He was along for the ride.

"'Cause, honestly, I'm getting really hungry," T-Rex said.

T-Rex had thinned down since leaving Sunnyvale, and he'd kicked his habit of picking his nose when he was nervous, but he still didn't look like an obvious fit to be a monster hunter. His round face, freckled nose and wide waist had made him a perfect candidate to be a Ratling at the Academy, working the kitchens and serving the food he loved. But as soon as I decided to seek out the five Jerusalem Stones from the five Creach Lords who had them, he'd stood right next to the others with his short sword clutched to his side, demanding that he come along.

"That much we can agree on," I said. "I think we're all hungry."

Xavier, the brainiac of our little group, gave a nervous glance to the boat's bow. "We better hope she doesn't get too hungry."

While most of the Black Guard relied on their swords, crossbows and other weapons to fight the Creach, Xavier's brilliant mind was a weapon in and of itself. He was only twelve, the youngest of our group, but his inventions had saved our bacon more than a few times already. His brilliance made him a little socially awkward though since he didn't see the need to filter anything that came to his mind. You never knew what was going to come out of his mouth. This comment about the last member of our group only said exactly what the rest of us were thinking but were too polite – or afraid – to say out loud.

My eyes flicked towards Eva, the proud fighter who'd been the first to tell me about this whole undiscovered world swirling around me. Eva, the fourth level monster hunter who was one of the most feared members of the Black Guard even though she only had one hand. Eva, the first girl who I'd fallen for but who wisely had kept us focused on our mission, which was so much larger than either of us. She was all these things, but since the events of the catacombs under the streets of Paris, she was one other thing as well.

She was Eva the vampire.

Her transformation was one of the reasons I hadn't slept in three days. Every time I closed my eyes, all I could see was Eva lying on the ground, covered with blood from where the evil vampire Pahvi had skewered her with a sword. It had been a wide, gaping wound. And it should have meant her death.

Only I'd made a bargain on her behalf. Every fiber of my being told me it was the wrong thing to do. That Eva would want to die with the dignity of a soldier. But, in the end, I was weak. I couldn't let her go.

With my permission, Shakra, the Lord of the Vampires and my aunt, saved Eva with the gift of her vampiric blood. In a whispered warning, Shakra let me know that Eva wouldn't only be a vampire, but she would be one of the most powerful vampires in the world. Gifted with the blood-gift directly by the Lord of the Vampires herself.

There hadn't been time for questions. The rest of the vampire horde chased us in an uncontrollable frenzy that even Shakra couldn't stop. As my group decided what to do next, our quiet conversations had only hinted at the most important question.

When would Eva need to feed?

When that time came, what would she eat?

So when Xavier blurted out, "We better hope she doesn't get too hungry," we all froze to see what Eva's reaction would be. The old Eva would have simply walked up, cuffed Xavier on the ear, and told him he was being rude. I hoped she would do something like that. I even wished she would get angry. Something. Anything.

But she didn't. She only continued to do what she'd done for the past three days – stand at the bow of the boat, staring forward at the swirling waters of the river, unmoving, wrapped in a cloak taken from one of the vampires.

"Nice one, X," Will said, punching him in the arm.

Xavier looked confused. "What'd I say? It's just a fact. She's a vampire now. Vampires feed to live just like we do. It's just a matter of time before –"

"We all know that," I blurted, cutting him off. "That's why we should go find Aquinas. See if she... I don't know... whether she can..."

"You know the law," Daniel hissed. "A hunter

who has been turned into a Creach must be killed or imprisoned."

"Great," Will said. "So you want to kill her or throw her in prison. Nice."

"Of course not, you little mugpug," Daniel said. "I'm saying that if we take her to Aquinas, that's exactly what will happen. I know Aquinas better than anyone here. She will follow the old ways."

"Guys, this is the same argument all over again," T-Rex huffed, sounding like a kid trying to get mom and dad to stop fighting.

"You said yourself that the Jerusalem Stones can change her back," Daniel said. "Then we go get the Stones as fast as we can. End of story."

I sighed. T-Rex was right; Daniel and I were right back into the same argument. The hard part was that I didn't know which one of us was right. Maybe it would be better to go find the Stones as quickly as possible. Take Eva with us so we could watch out for her. But she hadn't spoken in three days. She hadn't really even moved in all that time except to pull up the hood of her cloak during the day and lower it at night. I knew from dealing with vampires before that they could walk around in the daylight without a problem, so that didn't surprise me. But outside of that, this was uncharted territory for all of us.

"Eva is one of us," I said. "She will get special treatment. Aquinas will help her."

Daniel must have sensed the weakness in my voice. He jumped at my self-doubt. "You don't know that," he said. "These are dark times, and Aquinas will do anything if she thinks it's necessary to protect the Black Guard. She kept the truth about Ren Lucre from you. You'd think mentioning that the Lord of the Creach was actually your grandfather would have been important for you to know. What else has she lied to us about?"

I turned away so he wouldn't catch the expression on my face. At first, no one except Eva knew what I'd discovered in the catacombs. Shakra's revelation that she was my mother's sister had rocked my world.

I wondered if Aquinas knew.

If she did and hadn't told me, how could I ever trust her? If she didn't, how might she react when she discovered it for herself? Based on that, maybe Daniel was right, and the best thing to do was take our chances by going after the Jerusalem Stones by ourselves. I hated to say it, but I hoped Eva wouldn't get too hungry along the way.

I was about to say as much to Daniel when Eva turned around and faced us. We were so surprised at her sudden movement, after being still for so long, that we all just stared back at her. I was caught, as usual, by how beautiful she was. But on this night, her eyes seemed to burn from some inner fire. She cocked her head to the side like an animal listening to a distant sound on the wind.

Then she turned to me and whispered in a barely audible voice.

"They found us." She nodded to the sword at my side. "Get ready."

Chapter Two

Right after Eva gave us her warning, things went downhill in a hurry.

Clawed, scaly hands jetted from the water on the port side of our small boat and grabbed onto the edge. It was perfect timing, and my mind registered that as a problem. Someone was in command and had trained these Creach well.

A bigger problem was that our boat tipped precariously to one side from all the weight hanging on it.

I lost my balance and staggered down the slope to the port side, hit the gunwale, and nearly fell into the water.

As I leaned over the edge, desperately pulling myself back on deck, I got a good look at what we were up against.

At least ten gillmongers hung on the boat. If you've never seen a gillmonger before, just imagine what a half-man/half-fish would look like, and you have a pretty good starting point.

Humanoid in size and shape, they are covered in slimy, scaled, green skin. A single heavy, armored spike sticks out along each long bone, from wrist to elbow, elbow to shoulder, knee to hip. But it was their heads that really threw me off.

Though it wasn't an actual fish, it was close. Tight green skin stretched over elongated faces with gaping mouths and hardly any chin at all. The mouths all hung open, gasping for air in the foreign environment. They had rows of sharp teeth, too long to fit in properly behind the thin lips.

Huge eyes completed the fishy image. Big, black, lifeless discs the size of baseballs with no white to them at all.

Unfortunately for us, the gillmongers' bodies were muscular and wiry. This was going to be no easy battle.

"Jack!" Will shouted, grabbing my shirt and pulling me backward away from the edge.

Even as he did so, the gillmongers pushed upward. The boat rocked in the opposite direction, sending us flying against the starboard side. They continued like this, pulling, pushing, pulling, pushing, until all of us sprawled out on the deck, holding on for our lives.

Everyone except Eva, that is.

I glanced up and saw that she remained on the bow of the boat, watching us with an expression of only mild interest.

Then the rocking stopped... and things got really bad.

The hands on the railing disappeared, and for the barest second I felt a surge of hope that something had scared them off. But all they were doing was plunging to the bottom of the river to have a firm surface from which to jump.

In a small explosion of water, the first gillmonger burst from the river, soared into the air, and landed on the deck of the boat, cracking the old wood planking with the impact. Then a second and a third rocketed over. Soon, there were five gillmongers on our small boat, each gripping a short dagger in its teeth.

Daniel got his wits about him first. He was right next to me on the deck, and I heard him say, "Sorry, but no one gave you permission to come aboard."

He stood, produced his sword from his side and, with a battle cry, plunged into the enemy.

I jumped to my feet and joined him. The gillmonger in front of me greeted the downward thrust of my sword with his wicked little dagger. The collision produced a rain of sparks that reflected in the Creach's black eyes. But it didn't faze the monster. He pressed the attack, dagger flying, his mouth gaping open and shut as he moved.

"Enjoy your bath," Will cried next to me as he

forced the gillmonger he battled backward into the river.

In the split second I glanced over to see Will, I let my guard down just enough for the gillmonger I fought. He feinted with a direct knife thrust to my head. I blocked it easily enough, but my footing was off. When the gillmonger kicked at me with a webbed foot, I stumbled backward and found myself up against the pilothouse in the middle of the boat. On reflex, I ducked and felt the gillmonger's left arm fly just over my head. The Creach's spikes hammered into the wood on the pilothouse, trapping him there.

I used the opening and slammed my shoulder into his exposed ribs, churning my legs as I hefted him into the air. With a yell, I chucked him over the railing and back into the water.

A quick look across the deck told me we were in trouble.

More gillmongers were launching out of the river and landing on the boat. All of the guys were fighting hard – even T-Rex and Xavier double-teamed a gillmonger together.

But to make things worse, the slow current of the river had spun us around and was taking us directly toward a sand bank curving out toward the main channel. That's when I remembered that nobody was steering the boat.

We hit the sand bank with surprising force, the current carrying us faster than I thought. Everyone on deck, both hunters and gillmongers, lost their balance and fell. I used the opportunity to dispatch the nearest gillmonger with my sword, lifted his legs, and tipped him overboard. The body hit the sandbank with a thud and lay there, unmoving.

Too bad the sand around the body did move. Claw pinchers made of black, shiny armor rose up from the sand, snapping at the air. Big crustacean bodies followed, dozens of them appearing along the sandbank, each as big as a large suitcase.

"Pincer-crabs," Xavier shouted. "They can bite through armor. Be careful."

"I was planning on it," was all I could manage as the gillmongers redoubled their attack, savagely swinging their swords and body spikes at the nearest one of us they could find. Anyone except Eva, that is. They left her completely alone as she stood silently at the bow.

The pincer-crabs crawled from the sand straight at us. The sound of splintering wood filled the air as they tore away chunks of planking wherever they touched the boat. They appeared to be unstoppable and mindless, ready to consume anything that stood in their path.

This proved true as I managed to trip the gillmonger I was fighting. I kicked him toward the pincer-crab just coming over the top of the railing. In the blink of an eye, the crab grabbed the gillmonger by the arm, dragged him over the edge and back to the sandbar. The pincer-crab detached itself and fell on the gillmonger. I looked over the edge of the boat and saw the monster crab feeding on the body.

There was a scream and then I heard Daniel bellow, "Xavier!"

I turned and saw Xavier with a pincer-crab on

him, one of the thing's sharp walking legs impaled through his shoulder.

"No!" I shouted.

But there were four gillmongers between me and Xavier, and more springing from the water. Pincer-crabs crawled up the side of the boat. Daniel had lost his sword in the battle and now fought with his fists. T-Rex stood next to Will, waving a short sword in front of him as the creatures closed in. Will pulled at Xavier's arm, doing everything he could to keep him from being pulled over the side to certain death. Screams of pain and terror filled the air.

We were lost. This was the end of our adventure.

Then I felt a breeze as something large flew by me so fast that it was already past me by the time I raised my hands to shield myself.

Three of the gillmongers in front of me flew through the air and off the far side of the boat, their arms and legs cartwheeling out of control. The pincer-crab nearest me shattered into pieces like someone had taken a massive hammer to it. Slimy pieces of glossy black shell covered the deck.

The thing causing this wreckage paused for a moment, arms raised, muscles tense, lips pulled back to reveal two fangs in her mouth.

Eva.

Only it wasn't Eva, not really. It was her body all right, but her eyes were like those of a wild animal. She looked right at me, and I could have sworn she had no idea who I was at that moment.

The world spun back into gear and everything happened in fast motion. Eva whirled across the boat deck, destroying everything in her path. Gillmongers crumbled from her furious salvo of punches and kicks. She dispatched the pincer-crab trying to pull Xavier off the boat by breaking off its leg. She used that to spear one of the gillmongers before landing a brutal kick on the crab's body that cracked it in half.

Xavier fell to the deck, holding his shoulder. Will and T-Rex rushed up to help him, and Daniel took a protective position in front of them.

It wasn't really needed as Eva continued her one-person destruction of the Creach. Soon, there was only one gillmonger left. Eva struck him with a brutal kick to the chest, and the creature collapsed to the deck. She was on him immediately, fangs bared, closing on the Creach's neck.

"Eva!" I cried.

She cocked her head my direction and hissed. She looked just like the half-crazed, wild vampires we'd seen in the catacombs.

Eva launched herself at me. I had my sword but I didn't use it. I dropped it to the ground and held up my hands to ward her off. Even though my Change the night before my fourteenth birthday had made me incredibly strong for my size, I was no match for her. She pinned my shoulders to the deck with one of her knees in the middle of my chest. She hissed again, her teeth sliding out farther as she lowered herself toward my exposed neck.

"No... Eva... it's me...."

Her eyes were glazed over, driven by bloodlust.

"Eva... please... stop... it's me... Jack...."

I felt her hot breath on my bare skin.

"Your name is Eva... you're a fourth degree hunter of the Black Guard...."

A sting as one of the teeth broke my skin.

"You're not a monster... you're a monster hunter...."

Her body went rigid. She pulled back and blinked hard. Her eyes seemed to focus on me for the first time. Her hold on me lightened, but I held back the urge to throw her. I just lay there trying to sound as calm as possible.

"This isn't you... Eva.... Fight it...."

She took a shuddering breath and released me. She slid to the side to lean up against the boat railing, her chest heaving from the exertion.

Daniel approached us slowly, stopping to shove the last gillmonger off the boat. He glanced over the side. By the look on his face, I could tell the Creach attack was over. He looked from me to Eva and then back to me again.

"I told you, we need to find the Jerusalem Stones as soon as we can," he said.

"No," Eva whispered. "Take me to Aquinas." She closed her eyes and squinted in pain. "Please. Just take me to Aquinas."

I looked to Daniel, and he reluctantly nodded his agreement. I let out a sigh of relief. Even though I'd been arguing for days that we go find Aquinas, the truth was that she had gone into hiding after the attack on the Monster Hunter Academy. I had no idea where to begin looking for her.

Lucky for us, Daniel was one of the best trackers on the planet. If Aquinas could be found, he would be the one to find her.

Or at least I hoped. One look at Eva and I knew we had to at least try. I just hoped Daniel was up to the job.

Chapter Three

Even though Daniel never admitted it, I suspected he'd been trying hard to locate the remnants of the Academy ever since we left the place behind over a month ago. It was a sound strategy. If he could find them, it meant the Creach spies would be able to find them as well. Only that was assuming the Creach had anyone as skilled in tracking as Daniel. It was said he could track a sparrow flying in a moonless night. Obviously an exaggeration, but kind of poetical, and it gets the point across. He was good. He was very good.

But after two days, I was starting to worry he

wasn't good enough.

Aquinas had covered her tracks well. After the brazen attack on the Academy, the ancestral main fortress of the Black Guard in the French Alps, Aquinas made a decision to move the remaining monster hunter trainees to different locations. Part of her strategy was that no leader of any group would know the locations of the others. This would ensure that if anyone was captured and tortured to reveal the whereabouts of the other groups, everyone would remain safe. To this end, she had told them nothing about her own destination.

We'd abandoned the boat, too damaged by the pincher-crabs to be of much use, and made our way south toward Spain. Daniel knew of several safe houses used by the Black Guard in the Pyrenees, the mountains dividing Spain and France, and he thought that was our best chance to find Aquinas. We hitchhiked, playing the part of students on a European vacation, explaining away the sidelong looks at Eva with her hood up by telling people she was under the weather.

Along the way, Daniel disappeared for hours at a time, going to some tavern or coffeehouse along the way, checking for contact with other hunters. Even when he did meet another hunter, the information was slow in coming. Daniel reported that word of the attack on the Academy had gotten out, and all hunters now lived under a heightened sense of suspicion. He came back once covered with dried mud, rips in his clothes, and a fat lip. He explained that at one tavern, two hunters had tested him through a swordfight in the stables to see if he really was the fourth level hunter he claimed to be. Only after he'd bested them both with his bare hands, they'd grudgingly told Daniel the rumors they'd heard about Aquinas's whereabouts. But it was stale news, nothing he hadn't already heard from other people.

During this time, Eva had fallen back into silence. Somehow she seemed even more withdrawn than before, like she'd closed off the outside world completely and lived only in her own head. I found myself wondering whether this was her way to stop herself from attacking us. The vacant look I'd seen in her eyes when she was about to pierce my neck with her fangs caused me to shudder whenever I looked at her.

Part of me understood that the hunger I'd seen in her eyes couldn't have just disappeared. It had to be lying just under the surface, fighting to come out. I wondered if her blocking us out was the equivalent to someone on a diet choosing not to look at the piece of cake or the slice of pizza sitting on the counter nearby. I was used to the Creach wanting to eat me. It was hard to adjust to the idea of having to fear Eva.

"I think I found them," Daniel said proudly.

We were sitting near a rolling stream under the country stone bridge, the kind trolls always hide under to wait for their lunch to come strolling by. There was no troll under this one though. It did provide cover from prying eyes and the noonday sun. We hadn't seen Daniel since the night before, but somehow he'd tracked us to this spot, hanging over the edge of the bridge to look at us. I half-wondered if one of us carried a GPS tracker or something that he used to find us.

He flipped over and executed a flip to land on his feet in the middle of our small camp. I noticed Eva jerk her head toward him for a second but then look back down at her hands cradled on her lap.

"You think or you know?" I asked.

"Ninety percent sure," he replied. He held up his hand toward Will, who tossed him a protein bar from our stash of food. Daniel ripped it open and took a huge bite.

"What are the data points?" Xavier asked. When the rest of us gave him a quizzical look, he rephrased the question. "I mean, how did you figure it out?"

"When looking for something that can't be found, the trick is to look for the evidence of the thing and not the thing itself," Daniel said, obviously pleased with himself, his mouth annoyingly full of protein bar.

"Sure, everyone knows that," Will mocked.

"Uhhh... I don't get it," T-Rex said.

"When you track a rabbit, you don't look for the rabbit," Daniel said. "You look for signs that the rabbit exists. Once you know he exists, you look for direction, speed. Things like tracks, a tuft of hair on a bramble, droppings."

"Eww... you found some of Master Aquinas's droppings?" T-Rex asked.

Daniel's smile disappeared. "No, of course not, you idiot."

I suppressed a grin as T-Rex turned bright red.

"So, what did you find?" I asked.

"Aquinas has need for certain herbs and powders for her medicines and potions. I've been canvassing apothecaries, mostly hunter-types but some regs too, who would carry the items she uses. I picked up a trail yesterday. She was cautious, never buying too much at any one place, but enough to notice if you're looking for it."

"That's brilliant," I said.

"Great data points," Xavier whispered. "I should have thought of that."

"It's okay, genius," Will teased. "You can't save us every time."

"Awesome job, Daniel. How close are we?" I asked.

"That's the best part," Daniel said. "We were heading the right general direction. If we get lucky with a ride, we can be there well before sunset."

"That's the best news I've heard in a while," I said. "Okay guys, let's head out."

As the others gathered their things, I approached Eva, who still had her back to us. "Did you hear that? Daniel found Aquinas. We can be there by sunset."

She nodded and then slowly twisted her body so she could look at me. She kept her chin tucked to her chest so her face was half-hidden by her right shoulder. I watched her eyes flash to my hands. One was on the hilt of my sword and the other hovered near the knife at my waist. I moved them, not even I aware that I'd subconsciously put them there, but the damage was done. It was clear that I didn't trust her. Eva stood and stalked away, shooting me an angry glare.

In my mind, we couldn't get to Aquinas soon enough.

The landscape changed radically over the last part of our journey. Gone were the level fields with their well-tended stone fences, replaced with a more rugged terrain of wild rock outcroppings and stands of ancient trees. The packed dirt looked impossible to till, yet we passed small farms with plots for vegetables or rows of grapevine. This was a hard land, and I guessed it took hard people to live on it. A few hours later, thanks to the kindness of a few farmers who offered us rides, we found ourselves only two miles away from our final destination.

Daniel pointed down a dirt road that curved away out of sight behind a hill.

"Come on, it's not much farther," he said. "Eyes open, though. If I was in charge, there would be traps set along the road."

I hesitated as he said this, and I saw Will and T-Rex do the same. Only Xavier didn't seem worried. When he caught my look, he just shrugged. "I'm just following right behind Daniel. If there's a trap, he'll set it off, not me. What do I have to worry about?"

Daniel shook his head. "Thanks for the concern."

As we made the turn in the road, we saw two horse riders come at a gallop over the far hill in front of us.

"Into the bushes," Daniel hissed.

We all sprinted for cover and crouched low to

the ground. "I thought you knew this was the right place."

"I said I was ninety percent sure, didn't I?" Daniel replied. "Ten percent chance we're here too late and this place is overrun with Creach."

I pulled my sword. "Funny time to mention that part," I said.

We watched as the two riders came closer. The horses could not have been more different from one another. One was an enormous white beast, thick-chested and tall, all muscle and sinew. Its mane flew in the air as it ran. The other horse was chestnut, its brown coat shining like satin in the light. Shorter and stockier than the other horse, it carried its head high, showing off its cocky attitude. The riders were what drew my attention though. They stood in their stirrups, leaning forward over their horses' necks, arms pumping. The sight reminded me of professional jockeys in the middle of a high stakes race. As they got closer, I saw the tight braids of their hair and realized they were young girls.

I moved to step out from the brush cover and Daniel grabbed my arm.

"We don't know who they are," Daniel said.

I grinned. "But I'm pretty sure I know whose side they're on. Stay here in case I'm wrong."

I stepped out, stood in the middle of the road, and waited. The riders saw me and adjusted their course, turning toward my position. The ground shook as they drew nearer, the horses' hooves pounding the hard earth. The riders hardly flinched at seeing me, but I did notice the one on the chestnut horse reach back in a fluid motion and pull a bow from a sling on her saddle. I readied myself in case she decided to fire first and ask questions later.

I left my hands by my sides, trying to balance not appearing to be a threat while still being ready to defend myself. The two riders galloped hard until they were right on me, pulling up only feet away, their charges stamping the ground, whinnying loudly. The girl on the chestnut had an arrow nocked on the far side of her body, hiding it from me.

"C'est une propriété privée," the girl on the white horse called in French. Her brown eyes cutting through me. "Esta propiedad privada," she tried in Spanish. "English?" she finally asked.

"That would be great," I said. "But I think I got the point with the bow and arrow over there."

The girl on the other horse dug her heel into her horse's flank and spun around so that the pulled bow aimed at my chest. I saw that she couldn't be more than eleven or twelve, with bright blue eyes that flashed intelligence and a calm that I found unnerving. I was clearly not the first person this girl had ever pointed a bow toward.

"That's my sister, Emmy. I think you're making her nervous," the girl on the white horse said, her tone making it clear I wasn't making either of them nervous at all. "When she's nervous, her fingers tend to slip."

"They're feeling pretty slippery," Emmy said, her voice too cold and expressionless for my taste. "Not sure how much longer I can hold on."

"That's okay," I said. "I'll be able to dodge that

arrow."

Emmy snorted a short laugh. "Oh, I'd like to see that. Kelsey, can I do it?"

Kelsey, the one on the white horse, the older of the two sisters, eyed me cautiously. "Only a demon could dodge an arrow. Is that what you are, then? A demon?'

I shook my head. "We're here to see–"

"We?" Kelsey said, cutting me off. She pulled the sword from her side. "Where are they? I should trample you with my horse and crush you into the ground right now."

"Oh, I don't think you could do that," I said.

Kelsey dug in her heels and spurred the great white horse on. I don't know if her intention was to brush by me to give me a scare or if she really meant to crush me like she threatened, but neither happened. The big horse didn't move a muscle. In fact, it lowered its head and made soft nuzzling sounds. It stepped up to me and placed its soft nose against my chest, nudging up against my chin.

"Saladin, old boy," I said, rubbing the warhorse's nose. "How have you been?" I'd ridden him at the Academy, the same horse that had saved my life against the screechers. The same one I'd ridden against the dragons at the Monster Hunter Academy. The fact that he was here meant we'd finally found Aquinas.

The others stepped out of the bushes, and Emmy lowered her bow.

"I'm Jack Templar," I said. "Nice to meet you both."

The girls flushed with embarrassment, obviously recognizing my name. "Sorry, we were told to not let anyone near... no one... you understand...."

"It's all right," I said. "No harm, no foul. Now if you could just take us to –"

Saladin reared back, nostrils flared, and whinnied a high-pitched shriek. His eyes rolled in his head, wild. Kelsey held on confidently and rode him out as he bucked and twisted. The other horse did the same, nearly bucking Emmy of his back.

"Quiet, Flash," Emmy said softly. "It's all right, boy."

The words worked and after a few harrowing moments, both of the horses settled down, although their ears remained pressed flat to their heads and their skin twitched. Saladin especially looked agitated. I'd seen him maintain his cool while being chased by a fire-breathing dragon through the middle of a goblin army. I couldn't imagine what had him so spooked.

We all turned and saw that Eva had stepped from the bushes. Saladin was her horse, one of her closest friends. And he was terrified of her.

Chapter Four

"Jack! Good to see you, lad," Bocho bellowed as he wrapped me up in an enormous bear hug that lifted me off my feet. The head Ratling lowered me to the ground, his scruffy beard and long hair giving him a wild look, although his eyes remained full of joy and mischief. "You're not s'pposed to be here, now are you?" he asked with a smile. "Master Aquinas is goin' to 'ave a fit when she sees you lot."

Bocho made the rounds through our entire group, patting each shoulder or head as if to make sure we were real. When he came to Eva, he stopped short, the smile disappearing.

"It's okay, Bocho," I said.

Tears sprang to the big man's eyes. "Oh, lad, no it's not all right," he said with a trembling voice. "What 'ave they done to you, Ms. Eva? How could they do this to you of all people?"

Eva looked up from the ground and met Bocho eye to eye. She seemed confused. Suddenly, I realized she didn't recognize him.

Bocho noticed it too. "But I've known you since you were just a little girl. It's me. Bocho."

She squinted her eyes. After a few seconds, she shook her head and looked back at the ground.

Bocho appeared devastated at first, but then he stood up straighter and squared his shoulders. "Well, Miss, we're just goin' to have tah get you fixed up is all. "Jack, I'll take you and Eva to Aquinas. You others go into the main house and get some food. You look thin as skeletons. And you all could use a bath too."

"I'm coming with you," Daniel said.

Bocho shook his head. "Not smelling like that, you aren't. Besides, Aquinas will want to see Jack alone. I'm sure of it."

"What would you say if I told you I don't care much what Aquinas wants?" Daniel asked.

Bocho glowered and his face turned red. "Then I'd say you and me were goin' tah 'ave a problem, Master Daniel."

Daniel took a step toward the big man. "I'd like to see you try."

"Enough," I said. "It's been a long trip. We're all tired and on edge." I turned to Bocho. "We're a team. Anyone who wants to come with me can come.

That's just the way it is."

Daniel gave me a slight nod, acknowledging that he appreciated me sticking up for him.

Bocho looked uncertain what to do but finally threw his hands up in the air. "I liked it better when I could boss you all around," he grumbled. "Come on, then. This way." He trudged off toward a small barn set away from the farmhouse.

"Uhh… I think you guys have this, right?" T-Rex said, eyeing the main house. "I can smell the dinner in there. Rabbit stew?" he asked Bocho.

This brightened the big man's face. "Yes, one of my best I think. The vegetables came right from the garden this morning."

Will licked his lips, and I noticed Xavier looking at the house too. While they felt obligated to come with us to see Aquinas, I knew what they really wanted to do.

"Why don't you guys go get some grub," I suggested. "That way Bocho doesn't get into too much trouble for letting all of us come."

"If it would help Bocho," T-Rex said.

"Yeah," Will agreed. "Might be better that way, right?"

Xavier studied the other two. "Am I supposed to pretend to want to come too, or can I just say I want to go eat?" he said.

Will looked embarrassed but I just laughed. "Go on, save us a plate."

The three of them turned. Kelsey and Emmy, the two sisters who'd found them, were waiting to show the visitors inside. I turned back to see Bocho studying Eva intently.

"Come on," I said. "Let's go see if Aquinas can help."

The barn was a sturdy structure with a stone base and walls of rough-cut, weathered boards likely taken from the surrounding forest before chainsaws were even invented. I was certain it had seen over a hundred harsh mountain winters, maybe even two hundred, and yet it still stood defiantly in its spot, giving every indication that it would be there for an hundred more. In this way, it was like the person inside of it waiting for our arrival.

The door creaked open and revealed an interior very similar to Aquinas's workshop in the Tree of Life back at the Monster Hunter Academy. The open floor was divided into sections with furniture serving as the boundaries between areas. A mini-laboratory filled one area with tables covered with beakers and flasks. Glass tubing percolated with glowing fluids.

Another area was set up with her library, a replacement for the ancient books destroyed when the Tree of Life at the Academy had burned to the ground. The third area contained couches and chairs arranged where she could host groups large or small with just a few shifts. It told me that even in hiding, Aquinas was not letting the younger hunters get out of their lessons.

There were windows high up on the walls where a second floor would have been if the barn had a loft inside instead of open beams. The lowering afternoon sun lit up windows on the west side.

Shafts of light pierced through the barn interior like pillars helping to hold up the roof.

One of these shafts spotlighted a leather chair in the middle of the teaching area. Aquinas waited for us there, propped up on cushions, watching us. She rose slowly when we came in, and I noticed how much older she seemed since I'd last seen her.

It wasn't only her grey hair that seemed to float behind her because it was so thin or that her face was as wrinkled as an apple core left out for days in the sun, it was the way her every movement seemed to cause her pain. I felt a pang of guilt recalling the way she had saved my life by covering me with her shield during the goblin army's attack. She'd left herself exposed and paid for it with a goblin arrow in her shoulder. The wound that still gave her so much trouble from the arrow had been meant for my body, not hers. I crossed quickly to her so she wouldn't try to walk toward us.

"Well, well," she said, her voice sounding weaker than I remembered. "Looks like our super-secret hideout isn't as secure as I hoped."

I pointed to Daniel who stood a few paces behind me, his shock at seeing Aquinas in this fragile state clear on his face. "Daniel did it all. I doubt the Creach have anyone with his skill."

Aquinas raised the cane she used for balance and pointed it at him. "If anyone could find us, it would be you. What was it? A hunter with loose lips? Some kind of pattern when we made the journey here?"

"The medicine you purchased," Daniel said in a

low voice. "I recognized the materials you've sent me to villages to get for you before."

Aquinas shook her head. "Such a small thing. Well done. Well done, indeed." She coughed and winced from the pain. Bocho rushed to her side and lowered her back into the chair. Daniel and I exchanged worried glances.

"And now you both wonder whether I've bothered to take any of those medicines I bought?"

Daniel looked at the ground. "No... I..."

"I may be injured and sick, but my eyes still work well enough, I'll tell you that," Aquinas grumbled. Her eyes looked past us and sought out Eva, who remained in a shadow next to the door where we entered. "It seems I'm not the only one who carries an injury." She waved her hand, beckoning Eva to come closer. "Come here, child."

Eva didn't move.

Aquinas closed her eyes and lifted her head slightly, giving the impression of someone trying to catch a smell in the air or listen for a distant sound. Suddenly, Eva jerked backward and slammed her body against the barn wall hard enough that dust shook from the rafters above us. The columns of light took on new definition as dust motes danced through the air. I looked at Eva, worried. But she stood perfectly still. When I looked back at Aquinas, her eyes were open and they bore right into me.

"Tell me what happened," she demanded. "Leave out no detail, no matter how small or inconsequential you might think it may be. Tell me everything if you want to save her life."

Chapter Five

Telling the story to Aquinas in minute detail felt like reliving the horror all over again. When I described to her the decision I'd had to make as Eva lay bleeding to death on my lap, tears ran down my face. Saying it aloud, knowing Eva was listening to my every word, was one of the hardest things I ever did.

When I finished, I couldn't look Aquinas in the eye, choosing instead to stare at a spot on the ground in front of my feet. I wished a hole would open in the earth right there and swallow me whole. It would have been better than standing in that barn with Eva, Daniel, Bocho, and Aquinas staring at me, judging me.

The Templar ring I wore on my right hand grew warm at the thought about the hole in the ground. I remembered the ring had caused things to happen when I'd wished hard enough for them before, so I quickly cleared my mind of the image.

I flinched when Aquinas put her hand on my arm. I hadn't even noticed her stand up from her chair. She whispered the only words she could have said to make me feel worse than I already did.

"It is one of the great mysteries of life why we most harm those we most love." She gripped my arm. "But a mistake made from love is still a mistake. You should have let her die with her honor."

I started to reply, but I didn't know what to say. In fact, there was nothing to say. The act was done. Telling Aquinas I thought she was wrong and that I still didn't regret what I'd done served no purpose. Eva was not dead. So she wasn't quite alive, but at least she wasn't dead. I knew that given the chance to redo it all, I would make the same decision again.

"Can you help her?" I managed.

"I don't know. Leave us so I can see what can be done about it... if anything."

Daniel and Bocho protested this idea, saying it wasn't safe to leave Aquinas alone with Eva. I have to admit I had the same worry. But the old master shot us a look we'd seen before. She'd made up her mind, and there was no changing it.

Finally, we all trudged out of the barn, the three of us leaning up against the door the second it closed to listen for any signs of a struggle inside. But the minutes passed without event, and finally we walked to the main house and began our long wait.

That was over three hours ago. The sun that had lit the countryside so brightly now drenched it in reds and oranges as it set behind the mountains to the west. Lanterns were being lit around the property, and a large campfire was being built in the rear of the house where the young hunters straggled in. T-Rex and Will were there, talking to some of the hunters they knew from the Academy. They knew I wanted to be left alone with my own thoughts for a while.

I should have been famished, but I couldn't do much more than push the food around my plate, only taking a bite when Bocho came over to ask how I liked his rabbit stew. The truth was, even the one bite I did take made me nauseous. I almost lost it right there at the table. It was nothing to do with the food. In fact, Bocho was a master with a rabbit, some vegetables, spices, and a pot, but my stomach just couldn't take it.

I carried my plate to the trash and secretly scooped the stew out in case Bocho was watching. It was getting late, and I was desperate to know what was going on inside that barn, so I headed back that direction. To my surprise, I saw Aquinas standing at one of the pasture fences near the barn. She was by herself except for Saladin who stood with his massive head over the top of the fence accepting the old master stroking his nose. I jogged out to her.

As I approached, Saladin whinnied in greeting and stamped the ground with his right front leg.

Aquinas turned, pretending to have just noticed me. I knew better than that. Even sick and injured, I was certain she'd been tracking my movements since the second I left the main house.

"How is Eva?" I asked.

"She's dead," Aquinas said matter-of-factly.

I stopped in my tracks and felt my throat clench. I suddenly couldn't breathe. "B-but... wh-what..." I couldn't get the words out.

"No, not the way you're thinking," Aquinas said. "Although it would be no small mercy to put the poor girl out of her misery."

"I don't understand."

"What's not to understand?" Aquinas snapped. "Eva the monster hunter is dead. We're left with Eva the vampire, a creature not quite dead but not fully alive either."

I breathed a little easier, understanding now that Eva was still safe. "You weren't able to do anything for her?"

Aquinas shook her head and fell silent for a long time. I had the sense that she was angry with me, so I waited, knowing better than to pepper her with questions. Finally, she said, "The blood in her is strong."

"You've seen this blood before," I said. "In Gregor."

Aquinas flinched. I wondered if she suspected how much I knew. "So you met the old fool," she said.

"I watched him die," I said.

She didn't react at all, and that said more than anything. She was holding herself in such complete control against emotion that it was almost hard to watch.

"Did he die well?"

"He died a hunter of the Black Guard," I replied. "Battling the Creach to cover our escape. Without him we wouldn't have found the Lord of the Vampires and recovered the Jerusalem Stone."

I pulled the stone from my jacket pocket. It was nondescript, no different than a river stone, a little smaller than a tennis ball. Looking at it, I had a hard time imagining it held incredible power.

"I'd like you to hold it for me," I said, handing it to her.

Aquinas cradled it in her hands for a moment and then slid it into a hidden pocket in her clothing.

"He was a good hunter," she said.

"He was a vampire with Shakra's blood in his veins. The same blood flowing through Eva's right now," I said. "How did he do it? How did he control it?"

Aquinas reached out to Saladin, and the horse nuzzled into her chest as if feeling her troubled thoughts.

"Gregor was strong. A leader of men even before he was turned."

"You know Eva is just as strong," I said. "As a child she sawed off her own hand to escape Ren Lucre's prison so she could avenge her family. She's braver than any other hunter we have. How can you –"

"Don't you think I know all that?" Aquinas raged, her eyes bright with anger. "You dare to lecture me?

I raised her. Trained her to become the weapon she is. I know her ten times better than you."

"Then you know how powerful she can be," I begged.

Her face softened as she saw the pain in mine. "But don't you see? I know exactly how powerful she can be, and that's exactly what makes her so dangerous."

"But she –"

"She could destroy this entire camp if she chose," Aquinas said. "Or at least most of it before one of the hunters got a lucky shot on her from a distance. We wouldn't be able to stop her."

"She would never –"

"Eva of the Black Guard would never harm us," Aquinas whispered. "But Eva the vampire may not be able to control what she does."

She looked away, and the next words she said were barely audible. "And that's why she must be destroyed."

Chapter Six

I couldn't believe what I'd just heard. For a second I assumed Aquinas had spoken so softly that I'd misunderstood her. But when she turned to look at me, I could see I'd heard just fine.

"You can't mean that," I said.

"The needs of the many outweigh the needs of the few, Jack. You know this."

"There has to be another way. Gregor is proof –"

"Gregor was one out of thousands. Do you really think Eva is the first to be transformed? Sometimes it happens in battle. Sometimes the draw of immortality is too strong for a hunter to resist as they age. I'd be lying if I said I had not been tempted myself."

"With Gregor?" I guessed, recalling how the old vampire had spoken of Aquinas with fondness, and his comments about her youthful beauty.

Aquinas looked surprised, but she nodded. "Yes, he tried to convince me I could control it the way he had. With time and hard work. Using certain techniques. He tried to persuade me to use the gift to do good and fight against the Creach using their own powers."

"What stopped you?" I asked.

"Fear, I suppose," Aquinas said but then shook her head. "No, you know that's not true. It wasn't fear; it was jealousy. I knew that Gregor burned inside to exact his revenge against Shakra for what she'd done to him. But I also knew he still loved her in a way he would never love me. I was young, and that hurt me like I'd never been hurt before. I couldn't imagine living an eternity with that pain."

"But you thought you could control it," I said excitedly. "That wasn't the reason why you didn't do it. Gregor must have convinced you he knew how to teach you to control it."

Aquinas looked off to the horizon where the sun's last glow painted the mountain peaks in rich colors. She seemed lost in a memory, and I stood silently for as long a time as I could to let her relive it. Finally, I spoke up.

"If the roles were reversed, Eva would do anything, try anything, take any risk to save either of us," I said. "You know that."

Aquinas nodded. "Because she can be a fool about such things."

"You taught her. You said so yourself," I offered.

Aquinas laughed softly. "And sometimes the teacher is reminded of her lesson by the student."

"So you'll try?" I asked.

She drew in a deep breath, held it, then slowly let it out. "Yes, I'll try." She held up a hand. "But I will do it my way, without interference."

"All right."

"And if I think I'm losing control, and she's a risk, then I'll do what must be done."

I stared at her, unwilling to agree. "Shakra told me that the five Jerusalem Stones united could save her. Turn her back into… into…"

"A human," Aquinas stated plainly.

"Back into herself," I said. "So, while you work with her here, I'll continue my search for the Stones."

Aquinas nodded. "The quest remains the same even if the reasons for it have changed. We've heard there is fighting among the Creach, a battle for power amongst themselves. The rumor is that the Lord of the Lesser Creach has defeated the Lord of the Zombies. That means there can be two Jerusalem Stones in one place, only we have little information on where they are hiding."

"That will be useful eventually," I said, excited by the idea of two stones being in one spot. "But Shakra told me how I can find Kaeden, the Lord of the Werewolves."

Aquinas frowned. "I thought you might save him for later. Kaeden will not part easily with his Stone."

"I have to get them all eventually, so it doesn't matter the order," I argued.

"Shakra told you where to find him? I'm surprised she knew. The Lords are cautious, wary of each other as much as they are of humans."

"She didn't exactly tell me where he was, just where I could go to find out." I explained to Aquinas what Shakra had told me. She didn't bother to hide her disapproval of my plan, but she didn't try to persuade me against it. We both had what we wanted. I'd gotten Aquinas's commitment not to give up on Eva and bought myself some time to collect the other Stones. Aquinas had gotten me back on track for my quest to find the Stones as quickly as possible.

She held out her arm, and I took it to steady her as she walked toward the main house.

"We have struck a fair bargain," Aquinas said, making sure I understood that she realized we'd each used each other for our own ends. "Let us wish success on both of our endeavors."

I looked down and saw that she held out at metal cylinder in her hand. The truthsayer. A powerful relic from my last adventure, it had the power to tell whether someone was speaking the truth. Well, at least the truth according to the person you were asking. It was a good reminder of how different experiences and points of view could create different forms of the *truth*. It was a powerful tool, but a dangerous one. I'd given both the truthsayer and the Jerusalem Stone I'd recovered to Aquinas for safekeeping, and now she was giving it back.

"You might need this along the way," she said.

I took the truthsayer from her and paused. "Should I ask what you know about what really happened to my mother and father?" I asked.

Aquinas didn't betray any emotion. She stood silently, waiting for me to make my next move. I held up the truthsayer. "Do you know what happened to my mother?"

Aquinas nodded. I looked down, and the surface of the truthsayer swirled like liquid mercury. Small dots floated across the surface, organizing into a single word, *FACTUM*. She was telling the truth. I felt my heart beat harder.

"Tell me," I said. It didn't come out as a question, but as a command.

Aquinas shook her head. "No. Not yet."

"Why not?" I pleaded. "Certainly I've earned the right to know."

Aquinas put a quivering hand on my arm. "You have at that, Jack," she said. "But not now. Not yet."

"Why?" I demanded.

"I will tell you, I promise. Just not yet," she said. "It's for your own protection."

I looked down at the truthsayer, and the surface danced again until the surface formed into a different word. *FALSUM*. She was lying. When I looked up at her, I knew she could tell from my expression the word I'd seen.

"All right," she said. "It's to protect the rest of us. And that's all I'm saying."

She walked away from me, leaving the truthsayer in my hand, the word *FACTUM* across its front.

I pocketed the device and followed behind the old woman, trying to imagine what could possibly have happened to my mother that the truth could put the Black Guard at risk. It was another mystery layered onto my already confusing journey through this world of monsters and hunters. I wondered if I would ever figure things out. I wondered if I would ever really belong.

We walked the rest of the way to the house in silence. The faint sounds of music floated to us on the evening breeze. Behind the building, we found dozens of young hunters gathered around the campfire. The night air wasn't cool enough to need a fire. It was there for a more basic reason. The light pushed back the darkness, the flames giving off calming warmth and a pleasant smell that recalled better days.

The music was a single girl playing a violin. I recognized Kelsey, the girl who had ridden Saladin. Her brown hair was out of the tight braid and hung loose over her shoulders. Her suntanned skin took on the glow from the fire, almost giving her the look of a gypsy.

She played a slow mournful song, her eyes closed as if she were alone in the world. Her sister, Emmy, sat beside her, staring into the fire. Then she began to sing in a voice that was so clear and innocent, it caused tears to spring to my eyes. Not only was her singing beautiful, but it was laced with the same terrible sadness as the violin.

Whatever events these sisters had endured

together were too painful for words, so they put it into their music. The younger sister sang in a language I didn't know, yet I knew exactly what she sang about –loss and sadness.

I looked around the campfire and spotted Will, T-Rex, and Xavier sitting together watching the girls perform. Daniel was there too, but farther away, on the outskirts of the group. He seemed to be trying hard not to listen to the song, poking the ground with his knife.

The music took a turn. Both the violin and the vocals became defiant, the sadness overwhelmed by bitterness and anger. Faster and faster the song went. The bow became a blur across the strings. I realized my hands were knotted in fists.

Then in one final achingly pure note, the voice and violin combined perfectly, each complementing the other, stretching out for an impossible length. Then, the sisters let the note slowly dissolve into the night air until it was gone.

No one moved at first, so taken with the music. Finally, someone clapped, and the rest of the group followed suit. But it was a reserved response. Not because the performance wasn't brilliant – it was – but because we'd all felt the same way. This was a personal song for the two sisters, but it was a song for the new Black Guard as well. Built upon the foundation of terrible sadness was a defiance that would never end.

"They all feel it," Aquinas whispered to me. "The war is coming."

"They're ready to fight," I said, not quite

believing it.

"Maybe. Are you?" Aquinas asked.

I looked at my friends sitting by the fire, laughing with the others, enjoying a well-deserved break. I knew it would be pointless to try to get them to stay here and let me go alone on this next part of my journey. Not only that, but I knew now that I needed them and couldn't do this thing without their help.

I looked over to Aquinas and saw her searching my face for the real answer. It was impossible to lie to her, so I just told her the truth.

"I'm scared. I'm scared that my friends might get killed. I'm scared I might be killed. I'm scared that I'll fail and Ren Lucre will win and I'll let everyone down, including my dad and now Eva too." I took a deep steadying breath. "But to answer your question, yeah, I'm ready to fight. I swore to do my duty, come what may, and that's exactly what I plan to do."

It sounded good at the time, brave even. But the truth was that I had no idea how we could win this fight. The odds were stacked against us, our enemy had every advantage, and we'd lost Eva, our best fighter. I didn't know whether we would ever get to all the Creach lords, let alone find the Lord of the Werewolves, but I knew we had to try.

Sometimes trying is all you can do.

I just wasn't sure if it was going to be enough this time.

Chapter Seven

I was right. There was no discussion about whether the guys were going to join me or not on this next leg of our journey. I tried to push on T-Rex a little, arguing that Bocho could really use the help at the house. He laughed and told me he was coming whether I wanted him to or not.

So were Will, T-Rex, and Daniel. But yours truly had stitched together Xavier's wound from the pincher crab. While I'm pretty good with a sword, it turns out I'm not so hot with little needles, and the wound needed a little tender loving care from the people in the infirmary. He was disappointed, but I could tell he was looking forward to tinkering in Aquinas's new lab to create some new inventions. He promised a new explosive tip for a crossbow bolt that could take care of the vilest Creach out there.

Xavier also knew there were going to be two stages to our next adventure. One to find the location of Kaeden, the Lord of the Werewolves, and a second to track down the Creach Lord and capture the Jerusalem Stone he kept. Xavier made me promise to contact him somehow so he could join up with us on the second part of our adventure. I appreciated how sure he sounded that there would be a stage two. As the train whisked through the countryside, I wished I felt the same confidence.

It was the first time we'd embarked on a quest without Eva. I shuddered thinking of the last time we'd all seen her. Against Aquinas's wishes, we stopped by the barn where Eva was imprisoned to say goodbye and give her spirits a little boost.

The others had not been in the barn yet, so they didn't know what to expect. When we entered, Eva was crouched in the corner of her cell, arms wrapped around herself in a self-comforting hug. She rocked back and forth, muttering like a crazy person. When she finally noticed us, she hissed at us like a cat and pushed herself farther back from us.

"It's okay, Eva," I said. "It's just us. Jack, Daniel, Will, and T-Rex. We're not going to hurt you."

Nothing in her eyes told me she had any idea who I was. It was like looking into the eyes of a terrified wild creature. I couldn't help but wonder whether her mind was too far gone for her ever to return. I could see from the expressions on the other guys' faces that they were wondering the same thing.

"Eva," T-Rex said sweetly, pushing a chunk of bread wrapped in a thin cloth. "The Ratlings made some corn bread today. It's really good, and I know how you like... how you used to like..." His voice cracked and then trailed off as he started to cry. "We'll miss you," he sputtered and tore through us to get back outside.

The rest of us said our goodbyes, but it wasn't Eva in the cage, not really. It was a creature none of us knew. And that broke my heart. If Aquinas hadn't sworn she would try everything in her power to bring her back, I never would have left her like that. Even so, I couldn't fight a nagging sense that I'd let her down by leaving her behind.

Will rolled onto his side in the seat next to me, snoring away, a little bit of drool hanging from the corner of his mouth. I looked back and saw Daniel sitting in his seat, staring out of the window. Things had been tense between us since the catacombs. He'd kept his distance from me and answered my questions in as short a way as possible. If we were to be an effective fighting team, we needed to clear the air. I jumped out of my seat and slid into the empty one next to him. He looked at me oddly.

"What's wrong with your seat?" he asked.

"Will's snoring sounds like a mating call for a mugwump," I said, happy to see Daniel crack a smile. "Besides, I thought we should talk." The smile disappeared.

"Okay, you want to talk?" Daniel asked. "How

about you tell me everything about where we're going?"

"I did already. I swear it."

"Yeah, just like in Morocco, right?" Daniel said. "Or your private conversation with Gregor. Or the plan you made up with Pahvi in Paris?"

I knew all those things bothered Daniel, but each one of them was necessary to accomplish the mission. "Look, I get why those things upset you, but I've told you everything I know. I promise."

Daniel stared me down. He sniffed at me, which made a weird sound because of the fake nose worn over where his nose had once been. "So, we're traveling across three countries, exposing ourselves to all this risk, and the only thing we have to go on is that the Lord of the Vampires, the one that tried to kill all of us, gave you a ridiculous riddle, the answer to which we're just guessing?"

"Well, when you put it that way, it just sounds crazy," I said with a grin, trying to lighten the mood. It didn't help much.

"There's nothing else?" he asked.

"No, I've told you a dozen times. All she said was, *"Go to Omphalos, the navel of Earth. Justice and mercy establish your worth.* Nothing else."

Daniel looked down his fake nose at me. "And like I said before, different religions say the navel's in a different place."

Xavier says it has to be the Greek navel because of all the Creach activity at Delphi," piped in T-Rex from the seat in front of us. He turned in his seat and propped himself up on his knees so he was looking at us. "And he's super-smart."

"I'm not saying he isn't," Daniel said. "I don't know why people can't just speak in plain English. All these riddles are driving me crazy."

"What'd I miss?" Will said, joining us.

"Just reviewing the riddle and what it means," I said.

"I thought Xavier already told us," Will said. "The legend of Delphi says that the Greek god Zeus wanted to find the center of the earth so he let go of two sparrows, one from the east and one from the west. The spot they crossed paths became Delphi, the navel of mother earth."

"That'd be cool if there was an actual belly-button there," T-Rex said.

"I doubt there's a belly button," I said. "But hopefully there's someone there who can tell us where we can find Kaeden's lair."

Daniel still wasn't satisfied. "You know, Xavier told me there hasn't been an Oracle at Delphi in like a thousand years."

"Almost two thousand, actually," I said.

"So what makes you think there's going to be anyone there to help us?" Daniel asked.

T-Rex and Will nodded as they considered this.

"Not only that," Daniel continued, "but *justice and mercy establish your worth* sounds like a trial or something, doesn't it? Maybe a battle?"

Daniel was right. I hadn't really thought of it that way, but I should have. . "So, what are you suggesting?" I asked.

"Just that we go in with the assumption that this

is a Creach trap. We go in on our toes, weapons in hand, ready for anything."

"You're right. We go in like hunters, not tourists," I said. The train shuddered as the brakes were applied. We looked out the window and saw the world that had been streaking past us slow down. "We're here."

We hurried off the train. I immediately tasted the salt from the ocean on my lips and smelled jasmine and olive trees in the air. To our right, the Aegean Sea stretched out from the small rocky port shaped like a half moon. Brightly painted fishing boats moored there probably looked about the same as they did a thousand years earlier. Smoke wafted toward us from a nearby restaurant. The unmistakable smell of chicken cooking over charcoal carried hints of lemon and rosemary.

T-Rex walked toward the smoke like it was a leash pulling him. "This place seems great. Maybe we should get a bite to eat first."

I pulled him back. "Sorry, T-Rex, but we need to get to the Oracle as fast as we can."

"I admit it smells pretty good," Will said. "C'mon, Jack. We've had nothing but that horrible food of the train for two days. I want something that's not processed or fried. Besides, how far can we be from this place?"

I turned and pointed to the snow-covered mountain looming up behind us. "That's Mt. Parnassus. And that's where we're going."

Daniel eyes searched the train station on hyper-alert. I'd scanned the area too and hadn't turned up any Creach, but I knew Daniel had a better radar for them than I did. He noticed me watching him.

"Looks clear to me," he said. "For now."

"Okay, let's grab some chicken... for the road though," I added. "We'll eat while we hike."

Minutes later, I couldn't have been happier that Will and T-Rex had asked to grab some food. The dish was called souvlaki, big chunks of marinated chicken with spices, grilled over an open flame. It came with fresh bread cooked in a traditional stone oven. We ate as we walked through the small town, taking in the sights.

Rows of two-story colored houses lined each side of the steep cobblestoned streets. There were cars in the town, but not very many, and most of those were rusted with faded paint. Several of the upper floors had balconies decorated with flowers in hanging planters and sheets of cloth held out on poles so they billowed in the wind like flags.

"Pretty secretive location, huh?" Will said, jabbing a finger at a sign pointing the way with *Oracle of Delphi* written in about ten different languages.

"I guess looking like tourists is a good thing," T-Rex said.

A bus stopped near us and off-loaded dozens of new arrivals. They stretched and groaned as they shook off the bus ride from their bones. Many snapped pictures with their cameras. I pulled Daniel's arm. "C'mon, let's join that group. We'll stand out less that way."

Daniel scanned the new group for potential

threats. As he did, I noticed a little girl, a local by the looks of her, working her way through the new arrivals, her hand out asking for money. The tourists ignored her as if she wasn't even there.

"Yeah, I think you're right," Daniel replied. His words distracted me, and when I looked back, the little girl was lost in the crowd.

The group was large enough that nobody noticed four teenagers joining in. As we hiked upward, the guide in the front did his tour-guide thing and pointed out the sites along the way.

Since we'd committed to being with the group, I decided to make the most of it and listen to the guide to see if there was anything in his presentation for us to learn. Unfortunately, it turned out to be in German.

I noticed Daniel listening intently. "You speak German?"

"Sure. Don't you?" Daniel asked.

I shook my head and he shrugged.

"He's just covering the basics right now, nothing we don't already know. Zeus. Swallows. Gaia's navel."

"Gaia?" T-Rex asked. "Who's that?"

"It's the old Greek name for Mother Earth," Will said. I was always amazed how Will, who was failing out of middle school back home, knew so much about so many things. Will had always said he was a genius and just bored with school. I thought it was just an excuse to get bad grades, but since our adventures had started, I wondered if he'd been telling the truth.

The tour guide's voice rose and fell dramatically, and the German crowd *ooh*ed and *ahh*ed. Even Daniel looked entertained, a wide grin on his face.

"What is it?" T-Rex asked.

"Yeah, what he'd say?" Will added.

"Turns out there's another story about how this place started. The god Apollo faced a dragon here named Python. After a furious battle, Apollo defeated the dragon and threw him down a hole in the ground. It's said that the dragon's decaying flesh produces a smoke or vapor that gives the Oracle the power to see the future. Pretty sweet, right?"

"Sounds like Apollo may have been an original monster hunter," Will said.

"This place is going to be awesome," T-Rex said.

Then we crested the hill, and T-Rex looked like someone had just taken away his ice cream cone. The ancient ruins of Delphi spread in front of us, but it was mostly just piles of stone.

A couple of small sections of crumbling walls outlined where buildings had stood ages ago. A few miscellaneous pillars stuck up into the sky.

In the center, the Temple of the Oracle lay in ruins, a circular stone base with only five pillars remaining. Each was a different size, and none of them connected to a wall or ceiling. Basically, there was nothing left of it.

This was going to be harder than I thought.

Chapter Eight

We worked our way down through the ruins toward the temple. While the complex was larger than I thought it would be, with ruins sprawled along terraces cut into the mountainside, the temple itself was much smaller. In fact, I had Daniel use his German to double-check with the guide that the small circle of stones was the right place. He assured us that it was, shooting us a disdainful look, maybe for not appreciating the beauty of the place.

I appreciated its beauty. I just expected something more than a pile of rocks roped off from the public.

As we got closer, I could make out the layout of the old temple from the ruins. It looked like the temple had two distinct layers, an outer wall of pillars and a much smaller circle of pillars in the center. I imagined that either walls or cloth had closed off access to the inner circle for everyone except the priests and whoever wanted advice from the Oracle. Sounds impressive except that the whole thing was about the size of one of my classrooms back at Sunnyvale Middle School.

"It's kinda tiny," T-Rex said as if reading my thoughts.

"But it was built over two thousand years ago," Will said. "Think about it. This was built before Julius Caesar. Before the Coliseum in Rome. I think it's pretty cool."

"I'll give you that it's cool; I'm just not sure what we're supposed to find here," I said.

"The dragon legend might be something," Daniel said. "Since there's a Creach lair around here, maybe we have to prove ourselves in battle?"

I shuddered at the thought of having to face dragons again. Two of them had attacked the Monster Hunter Academy, and I'd gotten up close and personal with them before it was over.

"Come on, let's get closer," I said.

We made our way through the crowd of tourists toward the temple ruins. As we approached, the Templar Ring on my finger turned warm and began to quiver slightly. I clutched my hand in a fist and glanced around, expecting to see some kind of imminent attack.

Nothing.

"What's wrong?" Will whispered, picking up on my anxiety.

I shook my head. "I don't know. I just feel like something big is nearby."

"I don't see anything," Will said.

"Something wrong?" Daniel asked, doubling back from in front of us.

"Jack senses something," Will said.

Daniel nodded. Given our history, that was enough for him to go on high alert without asking any more questions. "Do you have a direction?" he asked.

I focused, feeling the ring turn even warmer in my hand. But I couldn't lock in on anything. The presence seemed to exist everywhere at once. Its intention wasn't clear either. It wasn't good or evil. But not neutral either. It seemed both good and evil at the same time, able and willing to be both depending on… depending on what? My weird senses couldn't answer that part of the puzzle.

A cry came from our left. In our heightened state of readiness, all four of us spun toward the sound, hands on our weapons.

A few of the German tourists were yelling, but one man in particular was raising a fuss. Barrel-chested and square-jawed, the big man looked like he belonged on a poster for the German Olympic wrestling team. He waved one hand in the air wildly to get someone's attention while the other hand wrapped around a little girl's wrist.

I recognized her. It was the same girl we'd seen

begging from the tourists when they first got off the bus on the village below. I didn't need to understand German to guess that she'd gone a little farther than asking for money. My guess was that the big German had caught her trying to pick his pocket.

"He's calling for the police," Daniel said, confirming my hunch. "Says the girl stole his wallet. Heads up, guys. This might just be a diversion from the real attack."

The way the girl struggled against the big man, trying desperately to free her arm from his massive hand, I didn't think she'd staged it. Suddenly, the big German howled in pain as the girl kicked him hard in the shin. He flung her aside as if she'd bitten him.

She was so light that she flew through the air, hit the ground, and rolled onto the rocks. But with the grace of a hunter, she sprang to her feet in one smooth motion and broke into a run. Right toward us.

The big German, his face so red with anger that it was almost purple, got his wits about him and chased after her. He bellowed German words that would probably have made me blush if they were in English.

I spotted four security guards closing in from either side, coordinating with their walkie-talkies.

The little girl ran right past us without giving us even a look. She ducked under the ropes keeping the tourists from climbing directly on the ruins of the temple and made a beeline for the temple itself.

The security guards and the German converged on the spot from different directions, surrounding her. She climbed the rocks and stood in the center of the circular temple. The guards yelled at her in Greek, waving her to come out. The German shouted the same way, injecting some broken English into the mix.

"Come… girl… out…," he shouted.

The security guards ducked under the ropes and approached the girl in a tightening circle, their arms out as if cornering a wild beast. By the look in the young girl's eyes, they pretty much were doing just that.

I wondered what could have happened to the girl to put her in this position. Where were her parents? Why was she begging on the street?

I suddenly had a powerful image of Eva as a kid, one hand missing and wrapped in bandages, begging for money, relying on the kindness of strangers to survive. Without the Black Guard, she might have spent her entire life that way.

In a coordinated move, the security guards closed in on the girl at once. I half-expected her to squirt out from the huddle of guards like in the cartoons and run away, laughing. But she didn't. Despite her kicking and scratching, the guards had her firmly in control.

The German cheered, and his friends who had gathered around him cheered along with him.

The guards walked the girl over to the German and held her in front of him. We pushed our way closer so we could hear. The guards spoke first in Greek, but the German just looked at them blankly.

"Speak English?" the guard asked.

"A little English," the German said. "I want my money back."

The girl spit at the German. "I didn't take your money," she said.

The guards gripped her roughly, speaking harshly in Greek. She replied back, venom in her voice.

"She says she didn't take anything from you," the guard said. "That she only asks; she doesn't take."

"Forty euros missing. My pocket. Gone," the German said. "She little thief."

The guards talked among themselves. One brought out a pair of handcuffs and readied them. The girl's eyes went wide at seeing them, and she struggled to get away.

I dug into my pocket and brought out my wallet. Opening it, I counted out the rest of our money. It only came to fifty euros.

"We need that," Daniel hissed.

"Not as much as she does," I said. I stepped forward. "Here," I called. "I'll pay the forty euros. Just let her go."

The crowd spun my direction, and I regretted making a scene. After all, we were supposed to be lying low. I should have waited until they led the girl away from the other tourists before making my offer. But the look of fear in the girl's eyes was too much to bear. They reminded me too much of Eva's.

The guards looked confused, so I stepped up and pushed the money in the big German's hands. "Here, there's your money. Now there's no harm done."

The German looked embarrassed. He held the

money at first like it was dirty, but he got over that quickly. He folded the bills and stuffed them into his pocket.

"Now tell them to let her go," I said.

The German hesitated and then nodded at the guards. "It's okay. No problem."

The guards let the girl go. The second they did, she sprinted away like a rabbit being chased by a hawk without once looking back.

"So much for *thank you*," Daniel muttered.

I watched the girl dart through the ruins until she disappeared. Something told me I would see her again. It turned out my feeling was right – I just didn't know how soon.

Chapter Nine

The ruins at Delphi were a bust. We did everything we could to get close to the temple, but after the whole episode with the girl, the guards watched us too close. None of us thought we were missing much though. The ropes allowed us to get right up the edge of the stones outlining the old exterior wall. From there, we could see into the inner chamber, if you could call it that. It was just an open area with five worn down pillars. There were no inscriptions. No magical hole in the ground. If something was supposed to happen here, it was taking its time.

We decided to go back to the town, have a bite to

eat, and wait until dark to sneak back onto the site to get a better look around without the guards. The town was set for the tourists with menus in English and ridiculously high prices for everything. We walked a couple of blocks away from the town center and found a local place where the food smelled twice as good and the prices were half of the tourist traps'. Since we were considerably poorer than we'd been this morning, I was happy we'd found something cheap.

"What do you think?" Daniel asked after the waiter put plates of fresh grilled fish in front of us.

"I think it looks great," T-Rex said excitedly. "The lemon garnish is perfect. Smells like it was grilled over a real charcoal fire. Ummm... tastes great too."

"That's not what I was talking about," Daniel said, shooting me a look. "What's the plan?"

"I thought we agreed to head back up there tonight," Will said.

"Based on what we saw today, anyone here think those ruins are going to suddenly reveal something magical to us tonight?" Daniel said.

Will took up my defense. "Maybe. We don't know, do we?"

"That place has been totally picked over by tourists," Daniel argued. "I don't know how anything could be hidden up there."

"I felt something when we first went up there." I said, lifting up the Templar ring. "This got warm and started to vibrate."

This quieted them down a little. None of us, including myself, knew how the Templar ring worked, but we respected and feared its power. The silence was broken only by the sounds of T-Rex scarfing down his food.

"Why didn't you tell us?" Daniel asked.

"Because it disappeared when we got there," I explained. "We walked around the entire site like three times, and it never came back."

"But it sensed something," Will added.

Daniel looked unimpressed. "Could have been a Creach nearby. Or something that happened miles from here that set it off."

I couldn't really argue either way. I had no more idea how the ring worked than the other guys did. It had come alive only a few times, and that had been in life and death moments. This was the first time it had vibrated. I didn't know how to interpret what that meant.

"You guys have to try this fish. It's awesome," T-Rex said with a mouth full of food. He pointed to my plate. "Are you gonna finish that?"

I pushed my half-eaten plate toward him. "Go ahead, buddy. I'm going to the bathroom."

I left them behind and heard Will and Daniel get into a heated discussion of whether we were wasting our time in Delphi. I couldn't help but feel like Daniel might be right.

The bathroom was in the far back of the restaurant, opening to the alley behind the building. As I walked back out of the room, drying my hands with a paper towel, I saw the little girl from the ruins run by at a full sprint. Two teenage boys chased her, calling out to her in Greek, laughing and taunting her. I could tell by their tone that this wasn't a game. Going back to Dirk Riggle at Sunnyvale Middle School, I really hated bullies. I ran after them into the ally.

The backside of the buildings weren't nearly as nice as the fronts the tourists saw. Paint peeled from the walls. Telephone and power lines crisscrossed between rooftops like cobwebs. There was trash on the ground from overflowing dumpsters, and stray cats hissed at me as I hurried past them.

I heard the sounds of a fight around the bend in the alley. As I made the turn, I was surprised to see the two teenage boys sprawled on the ground, knocked out. There was a flash of movement to my left. The girl darted down another side alley.

"Wait!" I called. "It's me. The one who got you out of trouble up at the ruins." I ran after her. "I just want to talk to you."

The alley she'd run down was narrow and dark with shadows even during the day. It was like the alleys in Marrakech where I'd tracked the djinn who kidnapped Eva and T-Rex.

There was a wall at the end, and for a second I thought it was a dead-end. Then I saw a door to the right. It swayed on its hinges, showing that someone had just passed through. I opened it cautiously.

"Hello?" I called. "I'm not trying to scare you." I thought of the two teenagers I'd seen on the ground and considered that this girl probably wasn't scared of me. She'd shown she could handle herself.

I peered inside and saw an unexpected sight.

A dark, high-ceiled room filled with men, wild

animals, and monsters.

All staring at me.

Chapter Ten

Muscular men held enormous swords over their heads. A lion, teeth bared, crouched ready to jump. A monster with a woman's body, but a head covered with snakes, held her clawed hands up, ready to scratch out my eyes. Winged harpies stretched their talons out toward me.

I would have been in big trouble if they had all been real. Luckily, they weren't. They were just marble statues.

Still, they were pretty creepy, an obvious warning to anyone dumb enough to break into this house that this was one place they really didn't want to be.

Beyond the statues, I saw the glow of natural light. I drew my sword and slowly made my way through the maze of statues. I remembered how the gargoyles on Notre Dame had come alive, and I wasn't taking any chances. Lucky for me, all the statues behaved themselves and remained frozen in place.

After I passed the last statue, a long, serpentine dragon with marble flames billowing from its mouth, I saw that the light came from a large, round courtyard garden, surrounded on all sides by windowless walls two-stories high.

Ornate columns lined its outside edges. In the center of the garden stood another circle of pillars. From this second circle, out stepped the little girl I'd been following.

"You said you possessed no intention to hurt me," she said, her voice and word choice oddly formal.

Her eyes bore into me. They were an ice-cold blue, almost to a point of looking otherworldly. I could have sworn her eyes had been brown when I'd seen her at the temple.

"I won't hurt you," I said. "I just wanted to make sure you were okay."

The girl laughed, but it wasn't a pleasant sound. It felt like she was making fun of me for some reason.

"Then why do you bring a weapon into my garden?" she said.

I realized I had a firm grip on my sword. I was about to lower it, put it away even, but something made me hesitate. Something was wrong here.

"This is your garden?" I said, lowering the tip of my sword just slightly. "Pretty nice for a pickpocket."

The girl looked down her nose at me. "I only ask. I do not take what is not mine."

"So you didn't take that German guy's money?"

The girl closed her eyes for a brief second and then opened them. "That idiot will find his money in his backpack tonight and feel only joy that he came out forty euros ahead. He'll laugh with his friends about the idiot American who gave his money to save a street beggar."

The Templar ring vibrated in my hand. The girl's eyes darted to it, and I covered it with my other hand on reflex. She smiled, but again I felt the sense that there was no kindness in it.

"So the rumors are true. You have recovered the Templar ring, and you collect the Jerusalem Stones."

"Who are you?" I whispered.

"I think you already know that, Jack Templar," the girl said.

"You're the one I came to find," I said. "You're the Oracle of Delphi."

The girl grinned and raised her arms over her head. Slowly, she transformed in front of me, growing from a child into a teenager, then a young woman. The baggy clothes of the girl became a well-cut dress, cinched at the waist by a red sash. The facial features bore a resemblance to the little girl but were now developed in real beauty. The eyes remained the same though. Ice-cold, calculating, pale-blue so they almost appeared clear.

"Yes, I am the Oracle. My name is Pythia. And your kindness to me today gained you this audience."

My brain clicked into gear. "So that was the test?" I asked. "Just helping a homeless girl? I think most people would help."

"Then you are a fool. Man is a cruel breed, able to overlook the plight of even the most helpless, even the needs of a child."

"Not everyone is like that," I argued.

Pythia shook her head, looking at me as if I was stupid. "Even your companions would not have given the money as you did. Admit it. You give your race too much credit, Templar. It will be your undoing."

I bit my tongue. I wasn't here to argue the nature of man. I was here to find the answer to only one question.

"Do you know where I can find Kaeden, Lord of the Werewolves?" I asked.

"I see everything," Pythia hissed. "I see the thousand pathways each one of your movements obliterates. I see the birth of a thousand new ones stretching out into time eternal."

"Sooo... is that a yes?"

Pythia snarled at me, the elegant beauty disappearing for a second to reveal a wrinkled, shrunken face of an old woman. "You dare to mock me, boy?"

The Templar ring grew warm once again on my finger. It filled me with foreboding. Danger was near. "I thought you can see the future," I said. "It's what all the history books say."

"I can see all futures," she replied, regaining her composure. "You were born with free will – I do not take that from you. I do not take what is not mine."

I remembered her saying that minutes earlier and at the temple with the German. "You don't take what's not yours, but you ask for it."

"Yes," she said.

"So, what do you ask for in return for this information?" I asked.

"Belief," she said. "Belief that you could be the One. Will you give it to me, Templar? Will you give me this thing that I cannot take?

It was a curious request, and I should have been more alert to the venom in her voice. But I was eager to get the information and get out of there.

"Sure," I said. "How do I do it?"

She grinned and nodded to the space behind me. "Just by agreeing, you've already done it," she laughed.

I spun around. The marble dragon I'd passed on the way in was moving, slowly at first, but gaining more agility and speed by the second. Its wide scales slid over one another as it slithered from the shadows into the light of day.

"This will be fun," Pythia said.

I didn't need to be able to see the future to see that I was about to have anything but fun fighting this monster.

Chapter Eleven

I drew my sword and held it in front of me, cursing my big mouth. I had no clue why my belief that I could be the One meant anything to her. Or how giving her that belief gave her permission to test me. Still, I should have seen that the Oracle was searching for a way to get me to agree to this confrontation. Obviously, she operated under some kind of warped system where she couldn't force people to do things, only accept what they were willing to give her.

And I'd just accidentally given her the fight she wanted to see.

This dragon was very different from the ones I'd faced before. I mean, even outside the fact that the others had been made of flesh and blood and this one still appeared to be made of stone.

It was smaller than the dragons at the Academy. Those had been like prehistoric creatures, the size of small buildings. This one was on more of a human scale, the head like that of a large lion, with a thick, serpentine body and long tail that tapered off into a nasty barbed spike. I took special note of that and all the other parts of the dragon's body that might kill me. Its enormous fangs, curved claws, hooks on its elbow joints and probably the ability to breathe fire.

Piece of cake.

"This is Python," the Oracle said. "Once faced by the god Apollo himself. Can you defeat him, Templar? Do you think of yourself as a god?"

"Uh, no. But I am pretty good in a fight," I replied.

She scowled. I guess she didn't like my sense of humor. And neither did the beast coming toward me.

The dragon let out a deafening roar, so loud that I opened my guard to cover my ears. This move was exactly what it wanted me to do, and it charged the second I did.

But I was ready. Covering my ears was just a feint to lure the monster in. I spun to the side and brought down my blade as hard as I could.

As the dragon realized its mistake, underestimating me, it bent its body away. Just in time. Still, my sword struck a glancing blow off the side of the dragon's body, sending a fountain of sparks into the air.

Pythia cried out, and I couldn't tell if it was concern for me or for the dragon. I sensed it was because she didn't want this contest to end too quickly.

The dragon took up a position on the far side of the garden, its body and tail swirling in the air behind it like a propeller. I think it realized I wasn't just some person off the street. I was a monster hunter, and this fight was not going to be easy.

I held my sword in front of me, pacing the area, getting a feel for the fighting surface with my feet.

"This isn't necessary," I said to Pythia. "Can't we just talk? If you have questions, I can answer them."

Pythia laughed. "We are talking. Everything we do is language. And you know the old saying – actions speak louder than words."

The dragon charged. There was no roar this time or any indication before the attack. Its speed was amazing. It was on me before I took my first step to brace myself.

I managed to duck just as the dragon's claws tore through the air over my head. It was so close that I actually felt my hair move. I thought I was in the clear, but the dragon's tail whipped at me and struck me across the chest.

I tumbled through the air and slammed into one of the pillars. On reflex, I jerked to the side and felt the dragon smash a claw into the column where my head had been a split second earlier. Shards of shattered marble stung as they hit my cheeks and arms. This was no idle match. The dragon was out for blood.

I used the next pillar to brace myself and get my bearings. Sliding behind it, I had at least a temporary shelter as I took stock of my situation. Turns out, it was even worse than I'd imagined.

All of the other statues in the courtyard had also come alive. They stood on the opposite side of the rectangle, arraying behind the row of columns, craning their heads for a good look at the battle. They seemed content for now to be spectators. I just hoped it stayed that way.

The dragon lashed out again, using its tail to whip around the pillar I was hiding behind. I jumped out of the way but felt a searing pain on the back of my leg. The razor-sharp point of the dragon's tail had sliced through my jeans and cut my calf. It wasn't bad, especially since I had so much adrenaline rushing through my system. But the living statues on the far side of the courtyard howled and shrieked with excitement. I realized with a shudder that they must smell my blood in the air. The last thing I needed was for those others to get carried away and join the fight. If they did, I was a goner for sure.

I needed to finish this fight. Fast.

I did the thing I knew no one expected me to do. I attacked the other set of statues.

With a yell, I sprinted across the courtyard, jumping over a swipe of the dragon's barbed tail. I ran straight at a white marble Minotaur, a monster with a muscular human body and a massive bull's head. The beast's eyes opened wide. It raised its shield and spear as I launched myself at it. But the

Minotaur was too slow. My feet hit its chest with a brutal kick that sent it stumbling backward. Most important, it dropped its shield and spear. Those were what I wanted.

I grabbed them, grunting from their weight, and turned back to the approaching dragon.

Just as I feared, the creature's chest was puffed up as if it'd taken in a huge breath. I knew what was coming next. Fire.

I crouched behind the Minotaur's shield as blue flames shot from the dragon's mouth. They hit the shield and streamed around it. The shield grew hot in my hands, almost too much to bear. Finally, the chance I needed showed up.

The flames stopped, and I heard the dragon suck in another breath. Yelling, I heaved the shield up in the air so it flew over the dragon's head. The ploy worked, and the creature's instinct was to watch the shield, raising its head and exposing its throat.

I charged, grasping the Minotaur's spear with both hands. Reaching the dragon, I rammed the spear into its throat. A grinding sound filled the air, stone sliding against stone. The dragon roared, turning toward me with a claw raised over its head to strike me. I was totally exposed without a shield or anywhere to hide. Hoping to absorb some of the blow, I raised my arms even though I knew it wouldn't do much good.

But the blow never came.

The roar stopped too.

Cautiously, I raised my head to see what had happened.

The dragon was frozen back into solid stone, the Minotaur's sword sticking from its chest now part of the statue. The rest of the statue creatures slowly retreated from their spots behind the pillars and moved back into the entry room.

An odd sound filled the air – Pythia slowly clapping for me.

"Well done, monster hunter," she said. "Perhaps you are the One after all. You have given me hope. This is a thing of great value."

I didn't want to tell her that I didn't think I was the One from the prophecy. Heck, I kind of hoped I wasn't. No one ever gave me a straight answer, but I got the feeling that the prophecy didn't end well for whoever turned out to be this magical One person. I decided to play it safe and keep my own doubts to myself. "Then I've kept my side of the bargain. Now will you tell me where I can find the Lord of the Werewolves and whether we can defeat him?"

Pythia closed her eyes and swayed gently from side to side. "I only see probable outcomes. You must do the rest. But most men are heathens. It's simple to predict their behavior even without the gift of sight."

"So can you or can't you tell me where to find Kaeden?"

Pythia closed her eyes for a long count and then reopened them. "I know where he is. Whether you can find him is a different matter."

"I don't understand."

"One can tell the lazy man how to become wealthy through hard work, but will it make a difference? Likely not," Pythia said.

"I'm not lazy."

"No, but you are reckless and consider it bravery. Will a reckless hunter be able to find Kaeden even if I give him a location?" Pythia closed her eyes for several long seconds. I was close enough to see her eyes moving behind her eyelids as if she was having a dream.

Finally, she cried out, and her eyes shot open. They tore through me and I thought I saw fear in them.

"You have many paths, more than I have seen in eons. In most, you and your friends all perish. In others, you simply fail and see the world crumble around you."

I swallowed hard. "Isn't there a path where I succeed?"

Pythia nodded. "Very few. Even in these successes, nearly all of them end with most of your friends dying. For you to succeed on your quest, you must walk a razor's edge at all times. Every little mistake sends an earthquake into the future, taking away more paths until only the terrible ones remain."

"Are you always this cheery?" I asked.

Pythia gave me a genuine smile. "There is a path where all your friends will live. If you leave here without knowing the location of Kaeden's lair, you will never find it on your own, and you'll be safe."

"But Ren Lucre will win," I said. "He will destroy the world."

"Yes," Pythia replied. "And if I tell you and you go and seek the lair, either you or one of your party traveling with you will surely die. All paths point to this fate – no matter what you do."

A pit formed in my stomach as I realized the choice Pythia had just given me. Turn and walk away, and my friends would live, but Ren Lucre's army would sweep through the world. Or find the Lord of the Werewolf's location and ensure the death of one of my team.

"Choose, Templar," Pythia hissed. "Choose now."

Chapter Twelve

I trudged back to the restaurant. I'd been gone for about thirty minutes, so I figured the guys would have started to worry about me, wondering whether I'd fallen into the toilet or something. But I couldn't bring myself to jog or run back. My stomach felt upside-down, and I could barely stay on my feet because of the nausea. My mind reeled from what had just happened. I beat myself up for the decision I'd made.

I saw Will in the alley behind the restaurant. On seeing me, he scowled at me like a puppy who'd run off without permission. He called back over his shoulder and yelled, "He's over here."

A few seconds later, Daniel and T-Rex ran into the alley. I made my way to them, my hands up in apology.

"I'm sorry. I didn't mean to worry anyone," I said.

"Where'd you go?" Daniel demanded.

I told them what had just happened, and they stared at me with open mouths.

When I got to the Oracle's prediction, I stammered. I don't know why, but I couldn't bring myself to tell them the whole truth. I wasn't ready to tell them the terrible choice I'd had to make – either let Ren Lucre win or accept that one of us would die chasing after the Jerusalem stone. It was one of the hardest choices I'd ever made.

"So?" Will said, "Did she tell you where to find him?"

I looked them each in the eye, one by one, and then nodded.

"Yes," I said, "I asked her to… and she told me."

They high-fived one another and thumped me on the back.

"So, where is he?" T-Rex asked.

"Here's what she said.

'Go into the darkest, most ancient of woods,
Where the knights of the Teutons lay rusting.
Defeat ye the lord through his champion beast.
Yet, in victory never be trusting.'"

"Ugh, I'm so tired of these riddles," Daniel groused. "Why can't these Creach just say it? I mean, why can't we get a simple 'head over ten miles south of such-and-such town, take a right at the big red barn, third spooky castle on the left' or something like that?"

"That would be nice," I said, only half-listening. I had to tell them how much this information had cost, but I didn't know how. I guess I was afraid they would be angry. They had a right to be. What business did I have making that kind of decision without asking them?

But it wasn't a true choice. Not really.

I'd fought against Ren Lucre before. I'd seen his power for myself, both in person and in a battle against a goblin army that was tiny compared to the coordinated attack he prepared against the entre human world. Aquinas's worry about him taking over the world wasn't some idle threat. He had Creach secretly positioned everywhere. In the police of every country. The armies. The governments. His Creach minions had infiltrated every seat of power, and all waited for his signal.

I couldn't just walk away and let that happen, right?

I noticed too late that Daniel was studying my face. By the time I caught him, he'd already seen the flash of emotion.

"What else did the Oracle say?" he asked.

I shrugged. "Not much."

T-Rex looked up expectedly. "Did she say anything about my grandma?" T-Rex had come with us only after his grandma had been taken away with dementia. He worried about her more than he let on.

"No, I'm sorry," I said. "I didn't have time to ask

her."

T-Rex's shoulders sagged in disappointment.

Will put a comforting hand on his friend's shoulder, but shot me a look. "She told you something though," Will said. "Something you don't want to tell us."

I nodded. Even as I made the choice, I knew I'd eventually have to tell them. They deserved to know. I guess I'd just hoped they wouldn't force me to do it this quickly.

"Out with it, Templar," Daniel said. "It can't be that bad."

"Oh, you'd be surprised," I said. "Okay, here it is. She told me that if she gave me Kaeden's location, it would send us on a path where one of us or all of us would die."

All three of them took the news in different ways. Daniel squared his shoulders. To him, death was just another adversary to defeat in battle. T-Rex sucked in his lower lip and chewed on it softly while he stared at the ground. It was Will's reaction that caught me off-guard.

After a few seconds, he burst out laughing.

We all looked at him like he was nuts, but he couldn't stop himself. He was red-faced, and snot bubbles kept appearing under his nose.

"What are you laughing at?" I asked. His laughter was so uncontrolled that it was infectious. Despite how terrible I felt, I found myself laughing with him. Soon, Daniel and T-Rex were too, although none of us could quite say why.

"Oh, my side hurts," Will said.

"Then stop laughing like an idiot," I said. "What's so funny?"

"You are," Will said, wiping tears from his eyes. "You were so serious and stuff."

I still didn't get it. "It is serious, Will. One of us, maybe more than one of us, is going to die if we keep going."

Will smacked me on the shoulder. "We all knew that when we signed up for this trip," he said. "It sounds like you're just figuring it out. You've got to admit that's kind of funny."

I looked around at their grinning faces. Will was right. We all knew from the beginning that this was ridiculously dangerous. We were lucky we hadn't all died three or four times apiece in the last couple of months. Still, part of me had started to believe we'd made it this far because we were somehow destined to make it through. That we were somehow invincible. Then again, Eva hadn't been so lucky.

The Oracle's prophecy made the danger feel all the more real. Like our lucky streak wasn't only likely to run out, but was guaranteed to. I frowned.

Daniel put a hand on each of my shoulders.

"If you're feeling bad that you made the decision without talking to us, just don't," he said. "If I was there, I would have done the same. All of us would."

"Absolutely," Will said, finally over his laughing fit.

Daniel and Will looked over to T-Rex, who jerked up a little when he realized it was his turn to say something. "Oh yeah, sure."

"Thanks, guys, I appreciate it," I said, really

meaning it.

"Uhh… is there a chance that she was wrong?" T-Rex asked. "I mean, nobody's perfect, right? She could be wrong."

"Let's make her wrong," I said. "Let's go face down the Lord of the Werewolves and show him what it's like to go up against hunters of the Black Guard."

"Now you're talking," Will said.

"So, where is he?" Daniel asked. "Where has the mighty Kaeden built his lair?"

"Well," I replied. "There's good news and bad news. The bad news is that we have another long train ride ahead of us."

"What's the good news?" Will asked.

I pointed at Daniel. "Unless I'm wrong about the Knights of the Teutons in the riddle being the Teutonic Knights, I'm pretty sure you get to use more of your German."

Chapter Thirteen

"The Black Forest is in the southwest corner of Germany. It's been the site for dozens of major Creach battles," Xavier gushed. "It has to be what the Oracle's riddle means."

He sat in the train compartment with the rest of us. He still moved a little stiffly on his right side, but he looked a lot better than when we'd left him five days earlier. Just as we promised, we'd sent him a coded message about where to meet us after the Oracle gave us a location. He'd met us at the train station in Austria loaded up with a backpack of inventions. These included crossbow bolts with enormous bulbs on the end of the shafts where the arrowheads usually went. Judging by the careful way he handled them, I guess they were the explosive tips he'd promised back at the farm.

"It almost seems too obvious," Will said.

"Did you know what it meant when you heard it?" Xavier asked with narrowed eyes.

"Well… no," Will sputtered. "Jack knew the Teutonic Knights were German. After I Googled it, I figured out where they lived."

Xavier looked disappointed. "Google's overrated," he said.

"Will has a point, though," I said. "Think about the riddle. *Go into the darkest, most ancient of woods. Where the knights of the Teutons lay rusting*. That seems pretty on the nose as being the Black Forest."

"And, *Defeat ye the lord through his champion beast. Yet in victory never be trusting*," T-Rex added, "… is just saying the way to beat Ren Lucre is through his champion, Kaeden the Lord of the Werewolves, right?"

"It does feel a little too easy," Daniel agreed. "She might as well have just said *Go to the Black Forest in Germany and kill the Lord of the Werewolves to get the Jerusalem Stone*. I mean, what's the point of speaking in riddles if it's so obvious?"

I remembered Daniel had complained about how complicated the riddle was when we first got it, but I bit my tongue.

"Maybe she adjusts her riddles based on how smart the person is she's giving them to," Will said, straight faced.

"Yeah, one look at Jack and she must have taken pity," Daniel added, snickering.

I threw my backpack at him and he broke out in a laugh.

"She probably would have drawn you a picture in crayon," I said, happy to be joking with Daniel. Things had been a little tense between us, and this felt normal again.

"Pointed you in the right direction and just given you a good shove," Will chimed in.

Xavier unfurled a parchment scroll and laid it on the small table between the two facing rows of seats. It was a map but unlike anything I'd ever seen in any of my geography classes back in Sunnyvale.

It was hand-drawn and looked ancient. The scale made it hard to identify at first, but I slowly picked out shapes I recognized. It was Western Europe but without lines for borders. I got the sense that this was probably because very few borders existed when the map was created. Still, I picked out where Germany and France filled most of the paper. There were intricate drawings of rivers, mountains, castles, and villages scattered throughout. Faint lines connected different features, some of them dotted and others solid.

Xavier pointed to an area just off the center of the map where many lines converged. "This is it," he said, tracing the lines with his fingers. "The reported wanderings of the Lord of the Werewolves as tracked and reported by the monk, Benedictine, nearly five hundred years ago."

We all leaned over to study the details. I looked

more closely at the drawings and noticed that each of them contained a grisly scene. A headless man in one village. A man with no arms running in another. In each one, there was a drawing of a wolf walking upright like a man.

"Eww," T-Rex said, pointing to a drawing of a wolf with a man and a woman sticking out of its massive mouth. "That's pretty gross."

"How did you get this?" I asked. "Aquinas's library burned down when the dragons attacked."

"Only part of her collection was up there. A lot of it was hidden in the caves," Xavier explained.

"Nice timing, Xavier. We could have just used this map and saved ourselves a long train ride to Greece," Will said.

"Not to mention a meeting with a particularly nasty dragon made out of marble," I said.

"No, no," Xavier hurried to explain. "This makes no mention of Kaeden, only that it was a werewolf. The archives are filled with this kind of stuff from the old days. It only became significant once you had the clue from the Oracle."

"Let me get this right," Will said. "This map shows a werewolf tracked by a monk five hundred years ago?"

"Four hundred and eighty-two years ago," Xavier said.

"Like I said, around five hundred years ago. But this could have been any werewolf, not necessarily our guy?"

"Right," Xavier replied. "But with the Oracle pointing to the Black Forest, there's a chance it is."

"And how big is this forest?" I asked.

Xavier closed his eyes for a second, then answered. "About the size of Vermont."

"Vermont? You meant like the state?" Will groaned.

"Vermont reminds me of Ben and Jerry's ice cream," T-Rex said, rubbing his stomach. "They should do a flavor just for us. Monster Mash."

Daniel and I made eye contact, and I knew we were thinking the same thing. It wasn't what ingredients should go into T-Rex's Monster Mash ice cream. If Xavier's hunch about the map wasn't right, then it was going to be a long slog to find the Lord of the Werewolves. And the trick was going to be to find him before he found us.

"How sure are you that this map is pointing us in the right direction?" I asked.

"I estimate at least a twenty five percent chance I'm right," he replied without hesitation. "That's not bad considering all the variables at work."

Daniel and I leaned back in our chairs. I expected Will to groan again, but instead he chuckled at Xavier's level of precision. "Well, that means there's a seventy five percent chance we get to be tourists for a day."

Xavier nodded. "Isn't that great? I've wanted to go to the Black Forest for years to study it, but Aquinas would never let me," he said.

"Why wouldn't she let you go?" T-Rex asked, his brows drawn together.

Xavier laughed. "It's way too dangerous," he said. "There are Creach hiding out everywhere in that place. Old ones too. There's one in particular –"

"Right," Daniel said, cutting him off. "I remember now. You have a weird thing for the Boros."

"It's not a weird thing," Xavier said defensively. "It's a scientific study."

"Bordering on obsession," Daniel muttered. He apologized after glancing at Xavier's hurt look. "Sorry, Xavier. I don't know how you can believe those old stories. They're just bedtime tales told to keep young hunters in their beds. I've made some of them up myself."

Will, T-Rex, and I shared the same confused look.

Daniel shrugged. "C'mon, you guys have heard about the Boros, haven't you?" he asked.

"No. I'm not sure I want to," T-Rex said.

"You tell it, Xavier," Daniel said. "You're the expert."

Xavier looked offended. "I don't believe in it, not necessarily. But I believe in science. There's reference to the Boros in every millennia for the last two thousand years. A massive creature that feeds off the heat of the Earth's core, that burrows through rock like a worm through soft dirt, that has two heads, possibly three, and that –"

"– can swallow little hunters who don't listen to their instructors in one bite," Daniel cut in. "It's a boogeyman. Nothing more."

"And he's supposed to live in the Black Forest?" T-Rex asked, nostrils twitching.

Xavier nodded.

Will looked up from the map. "How does any of this help us get the Jerusalem Stone from the Lord of the Werewolves?"

Xavier raised a finger. "I'm glad you asked. The mythology of the werewolf and the mythology of the Boros do have a link. I knew about this particular map because I'd come across it in my studies. Look here." Xavier pointed at a section of the map. The werewolf walking upright snarled at a blob of ink with the word carefully scrawled beneath it. BOROS. What looked like a linked chain connected the two images.

"Okay," I said, "so, what's the link?" I asked.

Xavier frowned. "I'm still trying to figure that out. There's nothing in the archives."

Daniel groaned, but I noticed that T-Rex still looked worried. The Oracle's prediction that one of our group wouldn't make it back from this adventure alive must have hit him harder than he admitted. I made a mental note to stay close to him.

"Come on," I said. "Let's all get some sleep. We'll be there in half an hour. It might be the last chance for a while to grab a little shuteye."

No one needed to be asked twice. We were all tired, both emotionally and physically. I wasn't sure what lay ahead of us, but I knew it would likely take all of our strength and test us in ways we hadn't yet imagined.

I stood to leave the compartment as the others made themselves as comfortable as possible. I signaled Xavier to follow me out into the hallway. Once there, I slid the door behind us.

"How's Eva?" I asked him.

"I told you earlier," Xavier said. "Aquinas said

she's progressing as well as can be expected."

"Yeah, but that sounds like what Aquinas told you to say," I muttered. "I know you, Xavier. I know you couldn't have resisted trying to understand the science of what Aquinas was doing to try to save her. What did you see?"

He stared out of the window and then at his feet. "Nothing. I didn't see anything."

I laughed. "You're not just a terrible liar. You might be the worst I've ever seen." Xavier flushed red. I put a hand on his shoulder. "If you think about it, it's a compliment. Lying isn't something you really want to be good at."

"It's just that Aquinas made me promise...."

I felt a lump form in my throat as the worst-case scenarios built up in my mind. Eva had turned insane, unable to handle the transition. She'd attacked Aquinas. She was dead. Not knowing was worse than anything.

"Is she... is she...," I stumbled.

Xavier broke in. "No, nothing like that." He sighed heavily and cast a quick look up and down the hallway where were stood as if Aquinas herself might be lingering in one of the shadows. "Okay, yes, I snuck into the barn to watch Aquinas. She caught me, of course. She always does. But she decided to let me watch."

"And?"

"And... it was terrible." Xavier shuddered. "Eva was in a cage; you saw it. She got worse at first. Like she had a terrible fever. And she prowled back and forth like a hungry cat. You could see it in her eyes.

The way she wanted to... you know... feed."

"Has she gotten better or worse?"

"It was bad at the beginning. Aquinas went in the cage with her, but I couldn't hear what they talked about. Aquinas did all the talking. For hours and hours. One time, Eva lashed out at her, and Aquinas had to raise her cane, like she was going to hit Eva. But she didn't. She just kept talking to her."

"Did it work?"

"It seemed like it," Xavier continued. "Eva calmed down. Stopped pacing eventually and crouched in the corner of the cage, panting like she was thirsty. I guess she was now that I think about it."

I grabbed his arm. "She's still Eva. She wouldn't hurt any of us. Don't forget that."

Xavier nodded but didn't seem convinced.

"But she's still safe?" I asked.

"I don't know," Xavier said.

"What do you mean you don't know?" I asked.

"Well, the thing is... the thing I'm not supposed to tell you..."

"Just spit is out, Xavier."

"Eva escaped," Xavier blurted. "Two days ago. And no one knows where she is."

Chapter Fourteen

We were all back together in the compartment and everyone was wide-awake.

"I can't believe you didn't tell us, you little weasel," Daniel said.

"Leave him alone," I said. "Aquinas made him promise. Made him give an oath as a hunter."

"Technically, I'm not a full hunter yet," Xavier clarified. "So I did have some wiggle room."

I shook my head, hoping Xavier would stop trying to help himself.

"Poor Eva," T-Rex said. "I wonder where she is."

"From the sound of it, they're lucky she didn't...

you know." Will bit the air.

"Will, really?" I asked.

"I'm serious," Will said. "We all saw her on the boat. She barely controlled it."

A German voice belched out of the loud speakers in the compartment. I stood, gathered my bags, and unfolded a small paper map.

"What are you doing?" Daniel asked.

"Looking at the route map. This train's ahead of schedule. We'll be there in five minutes." I held out the map in my hand. "There's another train a half hour from now heading south."

"We're not heading south," Daniel said softly.

Normally, I could read Daniel well, but it seemed he was speaking a different language. "What do you mean? We're going back to look for her, right?"

"You know we can't do that," he said, his overly calm tone really starting to annoy me.

"You can't be serious," I said. "She needs our help."

"The most help we can give her is to gather the Jerusalem Stones so we can return her to normal," Daniel said. "Besides, it would be like tracking a ghost with two days head start on us. Three by the time we got back there. Even I wouldn't be able to track her."

"I can track pretty well," I said.

Will shook his head. "Sorry, Jack. Eva was probably good enough to lose you before she gained her vampire powers. Now? You don't stand a chance."

"Wait," I said. "You're on his side?"

"It's not about sides," Daniel said. "It's about what's right. Besides, she probably doesn't want to be found. Especially by us."

"What's that supposed to mean?" I snapped.

"Think about it. We brought her to Aquinas and she ended up in a cage," Daniel said.

"It looked terrible," T-Rex mumbled. "Her all curled up like an animal."

I shot him a look. "I don't believe this," I said. "None of you are willing to go?"

The others turned away from me, unable to meet my stare. I felt guilty, probably guiltier than anyone else since I was the one responsible for her becoming a vampire. Part of me wondered if this was clouding my judgment, but mostly I just wanted to fight and make them see things my way.

"Where did Aquinas think she might have gone?" I asked Xavier. "She must have had some ideas."

"We sent out search parties," Xavier said. "Aquinas thought she might have gone after the livestock on the farms nearby. You know... because she was probably hungry."

Even though I ate hamburgers and chicken sandwiches all the time, the mental image of Eva going to a local farm to eat part of a cow or a whole chicken raw made me sick to my stomach. Maybe it was because I knew she was going there not for the meat but for the blood. I don't know why it made such a difference, but it did.

"Did she go there?" T-Rex asked.

"No," Xavier said. "There were no reports of missing animals or anything, so we looked in the forests. Down at the river. But she was just gone. Vanished."

A heavy silence fell over us, each of us imagining our own version of Eva out in the world, lost, confused by her new powers, trying her best to control her thirst for blood.

"Why didn't Aquinas want us to know?" I asked, the anger burning with every word.

"For exactly this reason," Daniel whispered. "She knew our impulse would be to go look for her."

"Maybe we should," Will said. Daniel looked at him sharply, and he looked sheepish. He avoided Daniel's gaze. "Maybe you're right, Jack. If she's out there, then she needs our help. Maybe we should we at least try?"

I nodded, feeling the tide turn my way. "Exactly. What if we don't try and she dies out there? What if Ren Lucre captures her?"

Daniel spoke quietly, staring at his hands. "It's taking everything I have to fight back the urge to just agree with you, to grab my gear, head for the nearest door, pry it open and jump out into the night. I want nothing more than to go look for her. To at least try even if it is an impossible task." He drew in a long, shuddering breath, then looked up at me, eye to eye. "But our responsibility is greater than just one person. It always has been. Even if that one person is Eva."

"I don't think ¬¬–"

"If she were here, Jack," Daniel said. "What would she tell us to do? I think we all know."

No one spoke because each of us did know the

answer to that question.

Will finally broke the silence. "She'd tell us to do our duty, come what may."

"And our duty is to the millions of people who might die if we fail," Daniel said. "Ren Lucre is too strong. He will destroy everything. We cannot fail. Period."

As he spoke, I remembered the moment I had with Eva in Spain the night after we had fled from the djinn in Marrakesh. Standing up high on a cliff, staring out together into the dark seas, she'd said many of the same things to me about our duty and our responsibility. I shook my head to clear away the memory, still not convinced.

"But this is Eva," I said. To me that was enough of an argument to counter everything he'd just said.

"We need to stay the course," he replied. "There's too much at stake here. Eva would have told us to keep going. She would have reminded us of all the people who had sacrificed to get us this far. She would have told us to think about your Aunt Sophie. To think of Hester. Gregor. My family. Her family. All the others who sacrificed for us. When it's my turn, if there's a choice to make, I will sacrifice everything to this cause. It is simply that important."

The train conductor hit the brakes as the train hit a rough section of track and jostled the carriage. The overhead lights flickered on and off, and the sound from the wheels masked the sound of the compartment door as I flung it open.

I raced down the hall. I had to get off this train as soon as I could. The air itself felt like it would suffocate me if I stayed a minute longer.

At the end of the hall, I wrestled the door open as we pulled into our station. The wind from the rushing train blew around me.

"Come on, Jack," Daniel called from behind me. "You know I'm right. She'd tell you the same thing and you know it."

I shook my head. "We can't just give up on her."

"We're not giving up on her," Daniel said. "Getting the Jerusalem Stones is the only way. If we save the world, we save her. Simple as that."

I stared at the ground slowly passing in front of me for a few long seconds as the train ground to a halt in front of an old-fashioned station. The small brick building looked abandoned. There was only one person waiting on the wooden platform, a figure in a long black cloak with a hood.

I heard the others behind me, and a quick check confirmed they had all of our gear. I grabbed Daniel's arm and leaned in close.

"Come on, I just found a way to settle this."

I stepped down onto the platform, and he followed. Soon, all five of us stood together on the platform. With a burst of steam, the whistle blew, and the train surged forward on its journey.

We stood together and waited for the last car to clear the platform and go clacking into the lightening eastern sky.

The figure on the far side of the platform hadn't moved since the train pulled in, but it didn't have to for me to know who it was.

She was pale and thin, her hair stringy, her

clothes covered with mud and grass stains. Her eyes were red and swollen, and they darted around as if tracking a fly in the air. But with all that, she was still the most beautiful sight in the world to me. Even with her vampire teeth sticking out slightly from her upper lip.

"Eva," I said, trying not to let my voice reveal the relief I felt in my chest. "About time you showed up."

Chapter Fifteen

Eva shuffled toward us like a stray dog used to being hit by strangers. Her slouch was gone, and most of the proud bearing of Eva the fourth degree hunter had returned. Still, pain pinched her expression, and she was barely holding back tears. Subconsciously, we all moved back to give her as much space to herself as possible. That's another way of saying we were all trying to stay as far away from her as we could. She noticed and smiled.

"What's wrong?" she said. "Afraid I might bite?"

There was a stunned silence until she gave a little smile to let us know it was a joke. I burst out laughing and so did the others. It was funny; but more important, it showed she was capable of joking. Something about her seemed *fixed*. She wasn't her old self, but she wasn't the creature huddled by herself in the corner of a cage either. Yet there was still something about her darting eyes that made me uneasy. She was hiding something.

"Now, if you're all done staring at me, can we get out of the open?" she asked. "This town is crawling with Creach. There's a tavern nearby where we can go."

She turned to go but none of us moved. She spun and faced us again, looking annoyed. As she moved, her cloak opened enough to reveal a Creach sword with a twisted handle made of tree root.

"Nice sword," I said.

"What? This old thing?" Eva said, her voice filled with mocking. Then in a blur of movement, she had the sword out from her side and her arm extended out to me so fast I heard the air *swoosh*. The point came to a rest less than an inch from my throat. Daniel and Will moved their hands toward their weapons, and I wondered whether I'd just sealed my death by allowing her to simply walk up to us.

No sooner had the question formed in my mind than Eva flipped the sword end over end. She grabbed the flat of the blade and extended the handle to me. I let out a breath and took it from her, marveling at the intricate design of the handle, which seemed every bit as hard as the steel embedded in it.

"Where'd you get it?" I asked.

Eva shrugged, her bloodshot eyes continuing to dart around feverishly. "I needed a sword. I found a hobgoblin who decided to give me his. Among other things he didn't need any more."

I shuddered at the idea that a hobgoblin may have been Eva's most recent meal. I turned the sword toward her and offered it back.

"Why don't you hold onto it for me?" she said. "Everyone seems a little jumpy. You might all feel better if I didn't have a weapon on me." She looked right at Daniel who had his hand on the handle of his sword.

I tried not to show my relief at the gesture. I simply nodded and held onto the sword.

Xavier blurted, "Where did you go? How did you get here?"

"I just followed you," Eva said. "Easy enough. You stick out like a blind fangworm at an Easter bonnet contest."

Daniel laughed. Up to this point, he'd kept silent, watching Eva with narrowed eyes. "They said you escaped into the woods. They were wrong, weren't they?"

"Of course," she said.

"Then where'd you go?" Xavier asked.

Eva lifted her chin toward Daniel. "Where would you have looked for me?"

"I'd have asked your state of mind first. If you were wild and deranged then I'd look in the woods. But you would have left a clear track in that case."

"Do I seem deranged and wild?" Eva asked.

Daniel shrugged. "A little bit, but you're here, so

you must have your wits about you." He sized her up. "You stayed in the barn," he said. "If your goal was information, then you needed to stay where the information was collected."

"So when I got the message from these guys to join them, you were in the room listening?" Xavier said. "That's kind of creepy."

"Not nearly as creepy as being locked inside a cage," T-Rex said.

"Thanks, T-Rex," Eva said. "Yeah, I heard you and Aquinas try to solve the riddle. Took you two longer than I thought it would. It seems kind of obvious, you know."

"A-ha!" Will beamed. "Tell me you had to Google it, Xavier. Come on."

Xavier was red-faced, but Eva gave him an unsympathetic look. He nodded his head. "We Googled it."

Will slapped his hands together. "I knew it. This is awesome."

Eva continued. "I wanted back in the fight, and I knew Aquinas would never let me leave, so this was the only way. I only heard the town you were going to but not what happened to you at the Oracle."

I gave her the short version of what happened in Greece with the Oracle. Eva listened, expressionless during the entire thing with a strange tension about her.. She raised an eyebrow when I told her about the dragon coming alive. I finished with the old soothsayer's warning that one of our group would die on the quest. She seemed to find the warning amusing.

"What's so funny?" I asked.

"I worried for a second that I might be the one who dies," Eva said. "Then I remembered I'm basically already dead."

This time no one laughed. There was an uneasy pause as we glanced back and forth to one another, unsure what to do.

T-Rex broke the silence. "You're not dead, Eva. You're just alive in a different way. And you always were, you know, a little different."

He said it with such seriousness that it didn't feel right laughing, but I couldn't help it. Holding it didn't help, and I gave one of those spitting guffaws that just kind of explode out when a laugh is held in too long. It was a chain reaction, and soon everyone was laughing except T–Rex and Eva.

"What? What'd I say?" T-Rex asked.

Eva smiled graciously, reached out her one good hand, and held on T-Rex's hand. "You said the perfect thing, T-Rex," she said. "Thank you. Besides, this whole vampire thing has its advantages too." She brought out her other arm from under her cloak, the one with the missing hand.

Only now, the hand was there.

Regrown and fully functioning.

She placed it on top of T-Rex's hand.

"You're the best of us, T-Rex," she said. "Don't you forget that."

Turning, she caught the rest of us gawking at her new hand. She held it toward us and wiggled her fingers.

Will leaned over to Daniel and whispered,

"Maybe you could become a vampire and grow your nose back."

"Shut up," Daniel muttered.

Eva looked at each of us in turn. "My name is still Eva. I am still a member of the Black Guard, a fourth degree hunter and the feared enemy of the Creach. Don't any of you doubt that, no matter what happens."

I nodded and hefted my bag onto my shoulder. I threw the Creach sword at her, hard. The way she used to do to me during our training sessions. She snatched it out of the air, spun it in an intricate series of swoops and slices, and slid it back into the scabbard she wore at her side.

"Okay," I said. "Who's ready to go find this Kaeden guy?"

"See, about that," Eva said. "I've been here for a whole day, walking among the Creach as one of them."

"And what did you find out?" I asked, afraid I already knew the answer from her body language but hoping I was just bad at reading the facial expressions of newbie vampires.

"Nobody knows anything about it," she said. "This place is a dead-end. I'm sorry."

Chapter Sixteen

After some discussion, we decided to try our own luck at finding out what people in town knew. Eva rolled her eyes but didn't say anything. We split up into three groups and spread out. T-Rex and Will stayed with me. Xavier and Daniel paired up. Eva insisted she go out on her own to work the Creach in the town once again.

With the exception of Eva, we looked the part of kids backpacking their way through Europe – except for the swords, daggers, axes, and mini-crossbows we hid in our bags and under our loose-fitting clothes. No one saw those, so we were okay.

As we split up, the skies to the east were tinted light pink with the day's first light, and I got my first good look at the landscape. It reminded me of my home back in Colorado. Great mountains stretched in every direction, more boxy than the craggy peaks of the Rockies but still imposing. The dense forest, mostly fir and pine, covered everything.

From the history Xavier had read to us, I knew most of the forest was new growth. Logging had torn down the ancient groves decades before. Still, the woods were lush and green. A wide river tumbled easily over smooth stones through the center of town, adding to a sense of peace in the area.

It did seem an unlikely place to find a Creach lord. I started to worry that I'd misunderstood the Oracle's directions somehow and that Eva was right. What if this *was* just a big dead-end? I had no idea what to do next except crisscross a forest the size of Vermont. That didn't exactly seem like a winning strategy.

"Sure this is the right town?" Will asked, his voice echoing my concern.

I nodded. "I don't think it's in the town, but somewhere nearby."

"Maybe someone in one of the restaurants could help us?" T-Rex sounded a little like Winnie the Pooh asking if there was a pot of honey around.

I nodded. "That's not a bad idea. We'll grab breakfast and try to meet some locals. Let's go with the story that we're students doing a research project on German mythology and see if that gets us any hits."

"Good plan," T-Rex said.

"You just like it because there's bacon involved," Will said.

"Absolutely," T-Rex said. "It's a proven fact that all plans involving bacon have a ninety percent better chance of working out."

We shared a laugh and headed for the nearest restaurant that showed signs of being open.

Unfortunately for everyone except T-Rex, neither bacon at breakfast nor bratwurst at lunch or strudel at dinner yielded a single lead. Not even so much as someone from the region who remembered werewolves in a childhood story. All we got for our troubles were some strange looks, a few laughs directed our way, and multiple suggestions that we spend our time visiting art museums instead of pursuing such foolishness as monsters.

Instead of being a hotbed of werewolf lore, the town seemed to be the one place in the world that had never heard of such a thing.

We met at the tavern we'd picked earlier as our rally point. Everyone was there except Eva.

"Hate to say it, but I think Eva was right," Daniel said, throwing himself into the chair across from me. "No one in this town knows anything."

"That's kind of what we found too," I said. "See many Creach?"

"Yeah, there are Creach all over this city," Daniel said. "Like ticks on a dog, they are burrowed in feeding off the humans here. All types. It's hard to believe the regs don't see them. They have to be able to feel that something is wrong."

"I saw pretty much everything except vampires today," Will said. "Except for Eva, that is."

"That's a good sign," Daniel said.

"What do you mean?" I asked.

"Vampires and werewolves hate each other," Xavier offered. "Always have. If Kaeden really was here, he would never let a vampire enter his town."

"I guess the fact that I'm still here isn't good news then," Eva appeared by my side so silently that I jerked out of my chair. "That and the fact I got nothing the entire day."

"Maybe Kaeden rules with an iron fist, and people are just scared to say anything," T-Rex offered.

"I don't know, T, you could be right, " I said. "But my gut tells me we would have found something today, no matter how small, if it were here to be found."

"Agreed," Daniel said.

The others nodded wearily.

"Tell me there's a plan B," Eva said.

I'd been trying to come up with a plan B all day, and I still didn't have one. "I've got nothing," I admitted. "I'm open to ideas," I said. "I'm willing to try anything that might get us to Kaeden."

Minutes passed, and we all picked at our food, no one offering a suggestion. Finally, it was too much to bear. "Come on, I don't think any of us can even think straight right now. Let's get a good night's sleep at a hotel with real mattresses and clean sheets and come up with a strategy in the morning."

Everyone mumbled in agreement. We paid the

bill and headed across the square to a hotel. Eva fell in line next to me.

"I know you're tired, but can you take a walk with me?" she asked.

My heart pounded in my chest. The way she'd said the words came the closest I'd seen yet to the old Eva, the one I'd gotten to know when she let the walls around her come down. Vulnerable and real. It was a quick glimpse of her completely back to being herself.

"Yeah... of course," I stumbled.

"Good," she said with a smile. "I don't really sleep anymore, and I feel like we should... you know... talk."

I called up to the others. "Guys, we're going to take a lap and check out a few more places. We'll meet you at the hotel."

Will and Daniel looked at us oddly, one from concern and the other with a measure of jealousy.

"Do you want me to come with you?" Will offered.

I shook my head. "No, we'll be fine."

Daniel looked back and forth between Eva and me, then turned and trudged up the street toward the hotel without looking back.

Eva reversed course and headed in the direction we'd just come, creating immediate distance between the others and us. I had to jog to catch up to her.

"Hey, who are we racing?" I asked.

She smiled, but it was thin and looked fake. This was the first time we'd been alone together since her dramatic return to our little group. I cleared my throat and was about to speak when she held up her hand to cut me off.

"The first time we met I made you a deal. Five questions and then we were done. Remember that?"

"Kinda hard to forget," I said, trying to get a read on her. The glimpse of the real Eva was long gone. The vampire I walked next to now seemed cold and calculating. "It was the moment my entire world turned upside down."

"Okay, we're going to do that again to clear the air without going on and on about things. Five questions and then no more, all right?"

"That's generous of you," I said, not meaning it.

"If I thought I could get away with no questions I would, but I know you too well. I think this is a better way. Do you agree to the terms?"

"Okay, let's do it," I said.

"Ask away," she said.

"And you'll truthfully answer anything I ask?"

Eva grinned, "Yes, and that's your first question. You really haven't learned anything, have you?"

"Wait, we're not really counting that, right?" I cringed as I said the words.

"Yeah, we are. And that was question number two. If you're really the last hope for the survival of the civilized world against the coming Creach war, the civilized world can officially consider itself in serious trouble."

"Thanks," I mumbled. "Okay, how does it feel, you know, to be a vampire?"

Eva took a deep breath. I could tell this was the

kind of question she didn't really want to answer. But this was her game, so she had to play.

"It feels like power coiled inside every muscle, and it takes total concentration to keep it in control. But keeping it in control makes me feel... how to describe it... like I'm tied up with every limb and muscle screaming at me to flex and stretch out."

She paused, and I knew she was hoping I'd burn another question with a follow-up. When I didn't, she gave me a little more.

"My hand growing back was unexpected," she said, flexing the fingers on her left hand. "I'd been without it for so long that it took a while to get used to it." She looked off into the distance. "My eyesight is so clear, it's like having binoculars attached to my head. I can hear things I shouldn't be able to." She nodded to a couple walking on the other side of the square. "If I focus, I can hear them from here just like I was standing next to them. I hear the butterfly flying over by that fountain. I can hear every drop of water like an explosion if I let it."

"What did Aquinas do to you?" I asked, knowing this was dangerous territory but also knowing the most dangerous question of them all lay ahead of me.

"At first, I couldn't control much of this. All my senses were bombarded the second I opened myself up to the world. It was like trying to take a drink of water from a giant fire hose. So I had to close down just to survive it. Aquinas taught me how to do that. Mind tricks, control exercises, meditation. It worked well enough for me to overhear that Xavier was going to meet you guys and to realize I needed to escape and rejoin the fight."

We'd walked through the square by this time and down one of the main cobblestoned streets. Old storefronts lined each side. I stopped and waited until she turned to look at me.

"Last question," I said. "Can you forgive me?"

There it was, the question I both didn't want to ask and absolutely had to ask. She didn't shy away from it but looked me right in the eye.

"I hated you for what you allowed Shakra to do to me. No, what you asked her to do to me. You turned me into the thing I'd spent my entire life trying to destroy. You put Ren Lucre's blood into mine."

"But you were –"

"Let me finish," she said. "And then we won't talk about this again." She drew in a deep breath. "I drifted into a dark place. So dark that I didn't think I wanted to go on. But Aquinas brought me back. She helped me understand why you did it."

"Do you forgive me?"

"No," she stated plainly. "I'm not sure I'll be able to that. But I don't hate you for it either. And that's going to have to be enough for now."

I nodded. Not exactly the words you want to hear from the girl of your dreams, but it would have to do.

"Those are your five questions," she said. "Happy now?"

"Not really," I said.

"Good," she said. "That makes two of us. But maybe now we can do our jobs a little better. We have a world to save." She pointed to a tavern in front of us, a dingy place with bad lighting and tilted walls. It looked like the place could collapse at any minute. A sign with a wolf walking upright as a man hung over the door, with the words *Heulender Wolf* beneath it. .

"That's German for the Howling Wolf," Eva said. "And this is our best and only chance to find Kaeden, so don't mess it up."

She strode toward the tavern without me. As I watched her go, I wondered why I liked her so much. I ran to catch up, curious about what I might find inside, completely unprepared for what would happen to me.

Chapter Seventeen

Based on the way the outside of the tavern seemed to be falling apart, I assumed the inside would be a mess. And I was right. Bare, dirty light bulbs hung from the ceiling in odd intervals, swinging slightly as the building moved with each step a patron took. A smoky fire burned in the hearth in the corner, casting weird shadows through the room. The plastered ceiling was low enough in places to touch with an outstretched hand. I noticed stains there, and at first, I thought it was from roof leaks above. On a closer look, the splatter marks were clearly from drinks thrown into the air. It wasn't hard to imagine a rowdy group of German fieldworkers getting carried away, clinking steins together as they sang the old songs.

A man stood behind an enormous dark wood bar, doing what barkeeps around the world do in their down time, rubbing spots off a glass with a dishtowel. He was thick-chested and bald, the top of his head as shiny as the polished wood of his bar. His eyes seemed too small for his face, an impression added to because he squinted like someone who'd lost his glasses. He wore pants and a long sleeve shirt mostly covered by a black leather apron like one an ironsmith would use. Although he avoided eye contact, he cast furtive glances at us from the first second we walked into the door until we reached the edge of his bar.

"We're closed," he said in a heavy German accent.

I looked around at the handful of other people in the place. Only five or six of them, but they were hunched over drinks, some eating plates of food. A waitress with dark red hair and fair skin came through the swinging doors from the kitchen, carrying platters of sausages and roasted vegetables. My mouth watered from the smell, and my stomach tightened to remind me I'd been neglecting it. The waitress, who I have to admit was very attractive, walked right past us and gave me a wink. I felt my face turn hot from embarrassment.

"You don't look closed," I managed.

"Really?" the man said, looking around. "You know what, you're right. Is this better?"

Just then, the waitress slammed the front door shut and lowered an iron bar across it. The other patrons jumped to their feet, knocking back chairs and tipping tables in their rush. Weapons didn't even need to be pulled, they'd been hidden under the tables.

In only seconds, a circle of swords pointed at us.

Even so, I pulled my sword and stood in front of Eva. I searched their faces and couldn't spot any signs of Creach among them. As far as I could tell, they were men.

Monster hunters.

They must have realized Eva was a vampire. They were doing what any good band of hunters would do – attack the Creach that had wandered into their lair.

"Put down your weapons," I yelled. "We're members of the Black Guard."

The waitress with the red hair stepped toward us. The circle of men parted for her to pass and then closed back behind her. I didn't know how I could have missed it before, but an air of command surrounded her. It was clear without a single word uttered or command given who was in charge here.

"I am Skyal," the woman said. "And how can a vampire-wretch like this be of the Guard?"

"She is," I said. "She's one of us. I swear it."

The men around us laughed. Even Skyal broke a quick smile, but it disappeared quickly. She was all business.

"Can you prove it?" Skyal said.

"The truthsayer, Jack," Eva whispered.

I nodded. "There's a truthsayer in my front coat pocket. You can use it."

Skyal glanced at Eva, then back at me. "All right, throw it to me."

I did as she asked, moving carefully in case any of them used my change in position as an invitation to attack. After taking out the metal cylinder, I tossed it to Skyal.

She caught it easily and rolled it over in her hands. "I've always wanted to see one of these."

"So you know how it works," I said. "You have to be careful to ask the right question."

"I know that," she snapped. "Do you take me for a fool?"

"No, of course not," I said, nervous that she suddenly seemed a little unsteady. "Just trying to be helpful."

"You can be helpful by answering this; are you a member of the Black Guard?"

"Yes," I said. Eva remained silent, glowering at the woman.

Skyal looked at the truthsayer, and I knew the tiny lines would be moving into the shape *FACTUM*, the Latin word for true.

"Good," she said, looking up from the cylinder. "Did you and the vampire here come to us with a secret plan to destroy us?"

"No, of course not," I said. "I didn't even know you were in here."

Skyal watched the answer form in the truthsayer and looked mildly surprised. "All right, last question. It's an important one. What's your name, boy?"

I hesitated, realizing that the woman didn't seem to care about Eva at all.

"I said, what's your name?" the woman hissed.

"Jack," I replied.

"Last name?"

"Templar," I said. "My name is Jack Templar."

The woman looked down at the cylinder and then smiled triumphantly. "Very good," she said, pocketing the truthsayer. "Thank you."

Even with Skyal's acknowledgement that I was telling the truth, none of the armed men surrounding us moved from their fighting stances.

"You have to believe me about my friend," I said to the group gathered around us. "She's one of us."

Skyal laughed, and the men around her followed suit. But it was an ugly sound full of hate and mockery.

"Poor fool," Skyal said. "You really have no idea, do you? I don't think I even needed the truthsayer to know that."

"What are you talking about?" I demanded.

"You're only half-right. Your vampire friend here is one of us." Skyal's eyes glowed red, and sharp horns grew from her temples, pushing through her red hair. "Only we're not one of you."

As my mind worked through the implications, I felt a bolt of pain on the wrist holding my sword. I dropped it, and it fell to the floor where one of the men picked it up.

On reflex, my other hand reached for the dagger on my side, only there was a hand on my wrist before I reached it. The grip was strong, holding me like solid rock.

I looked up slowly, already knowing what I'd see but not wanting to believe it.

Eva.

She had me by the wrist.

She was one of them.

"I'm sorry, Jack," she whispered. "But I told you I didn't forgive you."

I saw a flash of movement as her other hand smashed into the side of my head. And everything went black.

Chapter Eighteen

I didn't dream the first time. At least I don't remember dreaming at all. But I did wake up with a jerk, my heart pounding and adrenaline pumping through me. I thought I was coming out of a terrible nightmare. Turned out, I was waking up into one.

Thick ropes wrapped around me, binding my hands to my sides and my legs together in a bizarre cocoon. As if that wasn't enough, I lay in an iron cage being pulled along in a horse-drawn wagon. Trees streamed past me like a river. I had the uncomfortable sense that the world had lost its gravity, and things had simply spun out in every direction. The disorientation worsened when a face entered my field of vision from behind me, upside down and to one side. It was Skyal.

"Well now, you're not supposed to be awake, are you?" she said. Then she bared her teeth in a snarl. "Go back to sleep until we get there."

Another burst of white, hot pain to the side of my head.

Then everything went black again.

Chapter Nineteen

This time I dreamed.

I was flying over the forest, far above the height of even the tallest trees. I had the strongest sense of déjà vu and searched my memory for all the times I'd flown before.

There was a plane ride with my Aunt Sophie the year we went down to Disney World. The memory brought a smile to my face. Not just because any thought of my Aunt Sophie was a fond one, but because I knew now that as I'd ridden on the rides, watched parades, and soaked up all that Disney magic, I'd been right next to a devil-werewolf the entire time.

There was my airborne fight with the harpies when a group of them attacked us in the forests near my house in Sunnyvale. The view above those trees looked similar to what I saw beneath me, but I'd been holding on for dear life and then fighting and clawing my way loose after that. It was nothing like the smooth, floating feeling I had now.

The next time I flew was on the back of an outraged dragon flying over the Monster Hunter Academy and the surrounding mountains. That had been a wild, looping ride as the beast tried every trick in the book to shake me off its back and hurl me to my death. That experience had some of the power of the sense of flight I was experiencing, but still wasn't what I was looking for in my memory.

Then it came to me.

It was months before the ride on the dragon. I'd forgotten because it wasn't real. At least not in the physical sense.

The last time I felt like this was the night I'd drowned in the river escaping Ren Lucre.

The night I'd died.

The second I realized, I tumbled from the sky. I cried out, flapping my arms and kicking with my legs. The forest canopy rushed up at me, and I crashed through it.

Branches tore at my clothes, but they also slowed my fall. By the time I reached the lowest branches, I was half-falling, half-lowering myself to the ground. A few seconds later, I was standing on the forest floor on a soft bed of moss covered with dried pine nettles.

I took stock of my surroundings and reached for my sword only to find it gone. I was still wearing the clothes I'd been captured in.

Captured.

By Eva.

The memory of the tavern flooded over me along with feelings of betrayal and pain. Until that moment, the memory had the decency to stay on the sidelines, lingering right on the edge of my consciousness as if it knew it was too painful for me to handle.

How could Eva have done that?

But she hadn't done it, I told myself. The vampire blood in her had made her do it.

The words she'd used argued otherwise. *I told you I didn't forgive you.* Those were the words of someone enjoying revenge over an enemy. She'd said them with such bitter triumph that there was no way to explain it away.

Eva was with the Creach now.

A rustle of air through feathers whooshed right behind me. On reflex, I ducked rolled to my right, coming up in a crouched, fighting position. A white owl flew past me, easily navigating through the pine trees. It perched on a branch some distance from me and rotated its head until it stared at me with its oversized, black eyes.

"Hoo?" said the owl, making it sound like a question.

"Mom? Is that you?" I asked. I felt foolish asking, but the last time this had happened to me my mother had appeared. Still, she hadn't taken the form of an animal. She had just been herself.

The owl opened its wings and flew deeper into the forest. I ran after it, nearly losing it once or twice as it darted between the trees. The bright white stood out so starkly amid the greens and browns of the forest that sometimes all I saw was a flash of its color between the trees for only a split second. At first, I assumed the owl was leading me somewhere. But as it flew farther ahead of me, I considered that it was just trying to get away from me.

Just when I thought about stopping the chase, the forest opened into a perfectly circular meadow of tall grass. A slight breeze blew, and the grass swayed in a soothing, hypnotic rhythm. In the center of the meadow stood the five pillars from the ruins at Delphi, the Temple of the Oracle.

The owl circled once around the meadow, then flew over the pillars and flapped its wings in a controlled, slow descent into the center. I lost sight of the bird because the grass was too high, so I crept closer to the pillars. Slowly, the little girl I'd met at the ruins came into view, the form in which Pythia, the Oracle, had originally appeared to me. She smiled and walked to the edge of the circle formed by the ruined pillars but was careful not to cross over.

"You," I said stupidly.

The Oracle smiled. "You have a way with words, Jack. So eloquent."

"What are you doing here?" I asked but then realized I knew a better question. "What am I doing here? Did I... did I die?"

The Oracle laughed. It was an adult sound, disturbing coming from the little girl's body. "You'd like that, wouldn't you? Die and then come back like last time? Have that count as a fulfillment of the prophecy I gave you."

"The thought had crossed my mind," I said even though it really hadn't. I didn't want to let on that my mind was still whirling and having trouble catching up to this weird situation. The Oracle had proven to be dangerous. I needed to be sharp, so I didn't find myself in a battle with another one of her creatures because I said the wrong thing.

"Sorry to disappoint you, but you're not dead," the Oracle said.

"But the last time, it looked just like this. Felt like this," I replied, reminding myself that there was no reason for me to trust anything the Oracle told me. "How do I know you're telling me the truth?"

The little girl frowned. "Do you find insults an effective way to get people to help you?"

"Is that what you're doing?" I asked. "Helping me?"

The Oracle shrugged. "Maybe," she said. "Or maybe this is just a dream from that knock on the head your girlfriend gave you."

"She's not my girlfriend," I said, feeling slightly ridiculous saying it.

"Whatever you say."

"I think this is real," I said. "I mean, not really real, but I don't think I'm making you up."

"And why's that?"

"Because you're staying inside the pillars. I don't

think I would imagine you locked up like that. Somehow it's tied to you being able to communicate with me," I said.

"Aren't you a clever boy?" the Oracle said.

"So, you're here, but why?" I asked, more to myself than to her. "Do you want me to succeed?"

The Oracle shrugged. "I'm neutral on the subject. I can't stand the race of Man. Rude, obnoxious, greedy, a terrible waste of organic material."

"But you don't like Ren Lucre either," I guessed.

The Oracle scowled. "He wants to destroy mankind, which wouldn't be a bad thing, but he also wants to rule over us all. I can't decide which is more distasteful."

"Then we're back where we started," I said. "Why are you here?"

"I explained a little how prophecy works when I saw you last. Do you remember?"

"I mostly remember your statue trying to eat me."

The Oracle waved the comment away like a fly buzzing around her head. "Prophecy is not seeing *the* future, it's seeing *all* futures simultaneously and then trying to understand which outcome out of an infinite universe of outcomes is most likely."

"Like in a sword fight," I offered. "You have a hundred different moves to make and your opponent has a hundred different possible reactions, but you have to think them all through in a blink of an eye."

"I suppose so," the Oracle said. "Now suppose there are a thousand versions of you fighting a thousand opponents, and you get closer to what I see."

"Doesn't it overwhelm you?" I asked.

"That's why I remain inside these pillars. Even if they are erected only in my own mind, they protect me from being buried under it all."

I was starting to grow impatient. In the real world outside of this dream state, I was in trouble. Bound and captured by the Creach, being taken who knew where. Betrayed by Eva. Lost to my friends. As interesting as this little lesson on prophecy was, I didn't see how it was going to help me.

"Is there a point here?" I asked.

The Oracle hissed at my rude tone. I felt a little bad, but she did try to kill me once, so I didn't feel *that* bad.

"Once you left, I explored some of the most obscure potential paths your miserable little life could take. Buried there among the outcomes with the least chances for success was the possibility that you could fulfill the ancient prophecy of the last Templar. That you could bring balance back between man and monster."

"And why would you want that?" I asked.

"Because once that prophecy is fulfilled, prophecy itself will not be needed. My gift is my curse, and I want no more of it."

"How can it be a curse?" I asked.

"Think of it. Every person I have ever met, every person I have ever loved, I can see not only their deaths, but every conceivable way in which they might die. I've seen versions of your own future,

Templar, where you are skewered by a goblin's arrow, crushed underfoot by a tree giant, ripped apart by a pack of screechers, boiled alive in a witch's pot, burned at –"

"Okay, I get the idea," I said, not really enjoying hearing all the ways I might die.

"You see? I'm forced to see these and a thousand other deaths waiting for you whenever I open myself up to the flow of possible futures. I'm tired of it."

I heard the anguish in her voice and wondered how long she'd lived with the visions filling her head, with the pain of seeing every form of death for each person she met. I felt a wave of sympathy for her.

"I want nothing more than to succeed. For my friends. For my father. For everyone," I said.

Pythia looked as me hard. "And I want you to succeed for me. I will do something I have never done before and explain to you the riddle I gave you as your prophecy."

Then she told me something that would not only eventually save my life but also put me in the greatest danger I'd ever faced.

Chapter Twenty

I sat up with a start, shocked awake by the sounds of men yelling. I was still in the cage and still wrapped in thick cords of rope. We had stopped in the deep forest on what looked like an old dirt logging trail. Sunlight filtered through the canopy above, and I guessed it was midday, over twelve hours since Eva had betrayed me in the tavern.

I closed my eyes and tried to repeat what the Oracle had told me. I wasn't sure if it had been a dream or some kind of wacky hallucination from being hit too hard on the head... twice. But just in case, I wanted to make sure I remembered it.

Something small hit my cheek, and the Oracle's words disappeared. Poof. Gone. I opened my eyes just as another little pebble soared through the air and bounced off my forehead.

"Oops, sorry," came a voice from a nearby bush.

I couldn't believe my ears. It sounded just like T-Rex. But that was impossible. They were back in the town. No way could they be out here in the forest.

"T-Rex," I whispered. "Is that you?"

There was a long pause, and my heart sank as I figured I must have been hearing things. And dreaming things. But a guard came running from behind the cart my cage was on, passing by without giving me a second look, hurrying toward the shouting I'd heard farther ahead. This was no man, but a goblin with bulging eyes, hooked nose, and warty skin.

Once it passed, T-Rex's face poked through the bushes. He looked left and right for more guards, then scrambled out from his hiding spot. He didn't move with a lot of grace, but to me he looked like a Greek god sprinting to the finish line.

"Boy, am I happy to see you," I said. And I was happy – even though he'd knocked the Oracle's words right out of my head. If she was ever really there.

"Are you okay? You've been out for hours," T-Rex said, digging into a bag he carried at his side.

"I'm fine," I whispered. "Where are the others? Get me out of here."

He pulled a small knife from the bag and a plastic Easter egg. Sticking both through the bars of my cage, he put them into my hands, tied behind my back.

"Not yet. Hold tight. You'll know when to move," T-Rex said fast. He didn't wait for an answer, but turned and ran for his bush as if a pack of cursed demons was on his tail.

"Wait," I hissed. "Don't leave me in here. You can't –"

"Oy, you. Who you talkin' to?" a snarling voice said from behind me. I turned to see a goblin guard approaching, dressed in full battle armor including a spiky helmet. Over his shoulder, I saw Eva walking just behind him.

I slunk to the rear of the cage, cradling the knife and the weird little Easter egg between my hands and the small of my back. The goblin beat his spear against the metal bars of my cage.

"Oy, I'm talkin' to you," the goblin snarled.

Eva walked up and peered into the cage. Her eyes narrowed, and she turned and looked at the exact spot where T-Rex had hidden. She pulled her sword and crept toward the bush. With a lunge, she parted the branches.

Nothing.

T-Rex had been smart enough to get out of there.

"How could you do this to us?" I called out to her.

Eva returned to the cage and shoved the goblin aside.

"Don't you dare judge me," she said. "You don't know what you're talking about."

"This isn't you, Eva," I pleaded. "This is the

vampire blood. It's got you all messed up inside. You can fight it."

Eva laughed, and the goblin laughed with her, poking his spear through the cage at me.

"Fight it?" she mocked. "Why would I want to fight it? This feels great. I'm more powerful than I could have ever imagined. All of my senses are on hyperdrive. I can see in the dark. Smell my prey a quarter mile away. I can hear that mosquito on your neck drinking your blood."

I cocked my head to the side to shoo the bug away.

"This is where I belong now," she said. "This is my new family."

"No, your family died in front of you in Ren Lucre's dungeon, or did you forget?"

"I haven't forgotten," she hissed. "And now I have the murderer's blood flowing in my veins – thanks to you. You made me into this, and now you can live with the consequences."

"The Eva I knew didn't blame others or take the easy way out," I said. " Then again, I always wondered if the tough girl routine was just an act."

This seemed to get a rise out of her, so I pushed harder. "Everyone always talks about how brave you were to cut off your own hand to escape your bindings in Ren Lucre's prison. Maybe you weren't brave at all. Maybe you were just scared. So scared that you would do something like that to escape." I didn't know if I was getting through to her or not, but my anger was getting away from me. "Did you really see your family die there, Eva? Or did you run away and leave them like a coward?"

"Don't you dare bring up my family," she spit.

"What do you suppose they'd think of you now? Their daughter the traitor?"

"Should I make 'im bleed a little, miss?" the goblin guard asked, jabbing with his spear.

Eva snapped her head toward him, and I thought for a second I'd gone too far; she was going to have the Creach cut off a toe or two to shut me up. Relief flooded me when she shook her head.

"No, we have bigger plans for this one." She turned back to me. "If you know what's good for you, you'll shut your mouth. Right now."

The look in her eye was so venomous that I suddenly found it hard to swallow, let alone say anything. Even if I could have thought of a good smart-alecky response, I don't think I could have gotten it out.

"You'll regret those words someday," she said. "Wait and see."

Shouts erupted again from farther up the road. I craned my neck and saw at least two dozen armed Creach running toward us. Among them, I recognized the ones from the tavern, including Skyal, the redheaded woman with horns. The rest were a mix of goblins and ogres, dressed for battle. Looks of terror on their faces made them even uglier.

"What is it?" Eva shouted.

She didn't need an answer. Behind the Creach, a flood of giant wolves gave chase.

The Creach stopped in the road near my cage, some of them pointing and shouting what sounded like a warning in their guttural language, all of them looking in the direction they'd been running. I craned my head to see what they were looking at, but I already had a pretty good guess.

The rest of the wolf pack rushed at us from that direction.

In a short time, snarling wolves surrounded our group on all sides. They may have all been Creach, but it was clear that these two groups did not like each other at all. It felt like a fight was about to break out, and I was right in the middle of it, still tied up, in a cage and unarmed except for the little knife T-Rex had given me.

Bottom line, things didn't look good. And they were about to get worse.

Chapter Twenty-One

Skyal strode forward and addressed the wolves.

"We are here on the business of Ren Lucre himself," she shouted. "He will hear of this outrage."

The wolves didn't move. They either hadn't understood or hadn't heard the puny morsel of meat yelling at them. Carefully, I worked the little blade against my bindings, not knowing how much time I had before a brawl broke out.

Then one of the wolves let out a chugging sound from deep in its throat, almost like a cough. The others followed suit, and soon the sound filled the air. It took me a second to realize they were laughing.

Skyal looked unnerved by the response. Eva stepped forward and drew her sword. "She speaks the truth." She walked in my direction. "This boy is the personal property of Ren Lucre, your lord and master. It is of paramount importance that he be safely delivered. Any of you touch him, it'll be my steel you feel sliding into your heart."

Every wolf turned to watch me. Up until that point, I'd just been an unfortunate human being dragged along in the Creach caravan, probably for someone's snack later on. With Eva's pronouncement, I instantly became the most interesting thing in the forest. I glared at Eva, but she ignored me.

One of the larger wolves, this one with leather armor strapped to its back and chest, jumped down from the rocky outcropping he'd used to perch over us. On the way through the air, he transformed into a teenage boy, no more than seventeen or eighteen by the looks of him.

He landed gracefully on his feet and brushed back long dark hair from his face. I'd always thought Daniel was ridiculously good-looking, probably a source of my jealousy when Eva gave him any attention. But this werewolf guy made Daniel look like he was an old shoe. He was handsome, with fine features, soft eyes, and a body so ripped his six-pack looked chiseled from stone. The leather armor that had looked small on the wolf fit well on his frame, hanging down both front and back. With a smooth motion, his hands found cinches at either side of his waist that drew the armor tight to his body.

I couldn't help but notice both Skyal and Eva's appraising looks of this new form of the werewolf even as he walked past them. He ignored their raised swords with such confidence, it seemed impossible that either of them could strike at him. The werewolf crossed over to my cage and peered in at me, scrutinizing me from head to foot. Finally, he turned and looked at Eva.

"Why?" he asked.

Skyal flicked her hair to one side impatiently. "It's none of your business, now is it?" she said.

The werewolf held up his hand. "The next time the woman with the red hair speaks, my pack will rip out the throats of everyone here."

Skyal opened her mouth to reply but stopped short. The wolves around the perimeter bared their teeth, some of them drooling in anticipation. Skyal must've reached the same conclusion I did. This was no idle threat. They wanted her to speak just to have an excuse to attack. She closed her mouth and lowered her head.

"Good," the werewolf said. "Usually your kind are not smart enough to know when to stop."

"Not as stupid as a werewolf," came a high-pitched voice from among the Creach.

The werewolf spun around. "Who said that?"

The Creach looked around at one another, all pointing fingers at someone else. I bit my tongue because I recognized the voice.

Will.

I searched the crowd of Creach but couldn't spot

him. With the attention diverted away from me, I resumed sawing at the ropes holding me.

"Idiots, all of you," he said. He turned back to Eva. "But not as weak-minded as a vampire coming into the Black Forest," he growled. "There hasn't been one in these woods for centuries. None that escaped alive anyway."

"And why would that be?" Eva said. "Is not Ren Lucre the ruler of all the lands of the world?"

The teenage boy bared his teeth in the same way as the werewolves around us were doing. "Kaeden, the Lord of the Werewolves, rules this land," the boy said. "Ren Lucre and those loyal to him are not welcome here. He knows this all too well. A pity for you and your comrades here that he forgot to mention it."

"What kind of ruler sends out a boy to protect his lands?" Eva sneered.

The boy's expression turned from anger to bemusement. "What kind of lord sends a girl to find and bring an important possession to him?"

"Thinking of me as just a girl would be a mistake," Eva said.

"Then perhaps we are both at risk of underestimating the other," the boy said. He lowered his voice to a whisper. "But, just so we're clear, I suspect this is going to end badly for you and your friends."

"Lucky for you, I've decided to offer you a bargain," Eva said.

The boy grinned. "You'll offer me a bargain? By the gods, you are either the bravest or the most careless person I've ever met. I can't decide which."

Eva shrugged and gave the boy her most charming smile. "Well, I've never been accused of being careless."

He studied her hard for a few long seconds and then clapped his hands together. "All right, we'll make it interesting. Make me your offer and we will see where this takes us."

"I want to know where Kaeden is," Eva said immediately. "Take me to him so I can talk to him in person. Do this and I will let you live."

The boy erupted into a great bellow of laughter. The wolves around them howled and barked in response.

Skyal stepped forward. It looked like she was about to object to Eva's request. The boy glanced over at her, his laughter transformed instantly into a mask of rage.

"I dare you. Say something, demon," he growled. "Please."

The forest fell silent, all eyes on Skyal. She shrank down, shut her mouth, and backed away. The boy relaxed and turned back to Eva. I shuddered at the thought of how quickly the beast inside of him had shown itself. I made a mental note not to be fooled by the boy's looks. Violence coiled up inside of him like a snake ready to bite.

My hands were free from the rope, and I twisted carefully to work on my legs in a way that no one would notice. I hoped everyone was watching the verbal contest going on between the boy and Eva. Both the Creach and the wolves around us appeared restless. The beasts paced back and forth while the goblins, ogres, and other Creach all held weapons at the ready. It was a tinderbox that a single spark could ignite. I thought of Will's shouted insult. It seemed he wanted a fight to break out. I had to be ready for when it did.

Eva waited, expressionless, for her answer. The boy frowned, but it had an air of amusement to it. "That's an odd request," he said.

"I have a message for him from my master, Ren Lucre," Eva said. "Are you going to take us to him or not?"

The boy wagged his finger in the air. "Not so quickly. We're playing a two-sided game, remember. I want something in return."

"I told you, I'll spare your life."

"You mentioned that," the boy said. "But you bargain with something that's not yours to give."

"Says you," Eva said.

The boy waved the comment away. "I will take you to Kaeden in return for a simple thing."

"What is it?" Eva asked.

The boy stabbed a finger in the air toward me. "Tell me who that is," he said.

I breathed a sigh of relief. It was a simple enough thing to tell the boy a lie, that I was some kid picked up along the road or something. But then I remembered Eva had made a big deal about me being the personal property of Ren Lucre. So the lie had to be more convincing. Still, there were hundreds of options. I had insulted his name and needed to be punished. Or I had accidentally killed one of his minions and would be thrown in the dungeons. Anything would have been better than the option Eva chose.

"That's Jack Templar," she said without hesitation. I wanted to scream at her to shut up, but she seemed oblivious to the danger she was putting me in. "Supposedly, he's the last Templar knight, if you don't count his father rotting in Ren Lucre's dungeon, I guess."

The boy's eyes narrowed as he looked back and forth between me and Eva. "Jack Templar?" he asked. "The one who bested Shakra and destroyed Tiberon?"

"Destroyed Tiberon?" I blurted, thinking back to the massive black werewolf that had befriended me at the Monster Hunter Academy. "He was my friend. I lifted the curse on him. At his request."

"That's not the way I heard it," the boy said, turning to me. "The story I heard was that he helped you destroy the goblin army, and then you turned on him and used magic to destroy him."

"Then you heard wrong," I said. "If I had any magic, do you think I would be locked in this cage?"

The boy nodded, acknowledging the point. "Perhaps you're right, but you did best Shakra?"

"It's complicated," I said.

"But you took her Jerusalem Stone?"

I nodded. "She gave it to me of her own free will," I said.

The boy reached to the breastplate of his armor where a stone was mounted in the center surrounded by a design of metal flames depicting a sunburst. "But I will not give you mine. Not while I'm still alive."

Eva and I exchanged a quick look, the boy's words settling in on us. He saw our confusion and ended it.

"Yes," the boy said. "I am Kaeden, the Lord of the Werewolves. You are on my land. And now you both will die."

Chapter Twenty-Two

On Kaeden's last words, everything moved with blinding speed.

With a fierce kick, I broke through the last threads of my bindings and rolled free. I threw the plastic Easter egg T-Rex had given me at the door on the far end of the cage. Covering my head with my arms, I flew back as the entire end of the steel cage blew out. The explosion knocked the whole thing off the wagon.

The forest whirled past as I bounced around inside the cage. As fast as I could, I climbed out through the tangled mass of hot metal. A raging battle greeted me.

The wolves had fallen onto the Creach from all sides, but they were well trained and putting up a fight.

I searched for Eva in the mix and saw her matching swords with Kaeden himself. In only a few strokes, he had her on the defensive, backing her up on uneven ground. A fallen goblin lay right in her path.

"Eva!" I shouted.

Too late. She hit the obstacle with her heel as she retreated and still adjusted perfectly. Against probably any other opponent, the quarter-second hesitation would have meant nothing. For the Lord of the Werewolves, it was the only opening he needed. He stabbed her in the leg first and then slammed her head with the hilt of his sword, knocking her out.

Skyal pounced on him with a terrifying shriek, backed by two ogres wielding spiked metal balls on the end of chains. Kaeden engaged them, leaving Eva where she fell.

An arm grabbed me, and I spun around with T-Rex's tiny knife. Daniel and Will stood there, worried looks on their faces. Will threw me my sword.

"Eva," Will said.

I nodded. "I saw. Come on."

The three of us sprinted through the battle raging between the Lesser Creach and the werewolves. An ogre with a werewolf clawing his back ran between us, and we had to shove the battling creatures out of the way. I slid on the ground next to Eva. Lifting her head, I had a terrible flashback of holding her in the same way in the catacombs in Paris. For a second, the sounds of the battle raging around us faded, and I was just there with Eva.

Only this time, her eyes bolted open. It took her a beat to get her bearings, but once she did, she frowned at me.

"Let me go," she snarled. She pushed me away and stood up, her injury already healed. Grabbing her sword, she sliced it through the air.

Daniel and Will stood guard over our position, facing out. Their backs were exposed to Eva's blade. "Watch out, guys," I yelled. "Eva's with them."

"Don't be an idiot," Daniel said. "How do you think we tracked you here?"

I stared at Eva, dumbfounded.

"You?" I asked, my head spinning. "So you're not... you never were..."

"Come on, you can wallow in your guilt later. The Lord of the Werewolves is out in the open. The Jerusalem Stone is right there," Eva said. "This is our chance. Guard me."

She launched herself forward, moving so fast it was hard to tell whether she even touched the ground.

"Come on, guys," I yelled as I charged after her, right toward where Kaeden fought two ogres and three goblins simultaneously.

Eva reached the battle first, jumping onto the back of one of the ogres who was bent over, using the creature to catapult herself into the air high above Kaeden. With a cry, she swung her sword with her right hand while her left hand sliced low with a dagger.

Kaeden rolled to the side, ducking the onslaught. In the time it took him to roll, he transformed into a werewolf. The beast crouched down and jumped at the three goblins, wiping them out with one swipe. The sound of bones snapping didn't even slow him..

Eva gave chase, and I swung out wide to the other side so we would attack from two different angles. We had executed this maneuver a hundred times before, but never with her new powers. And never against anyone like Kaeden.

I spotted a troll's shield on the ground and scooped it up on a full sprint. Lucky I did because Kaeden swatted at my head, and I lifted the shield just in time to take the impact. The power behind it was incredible. It tore me from my feet and sent me flying until I slammed into a tree trunk and sagged to the ground. When I staggered back up, I saw that the shield was nearly folded in half from the blow.

Kaeden transformed again, not losing a step at he ran toward me. Daniel and Will surged forward to block the werewolf's path. Barehanded, Kaeden took them on.

In the first second, Kaeden ripped Will's sword from his hands. In the next second, he swept Daniel off his feet to land sprawled on the forest floor. Then he spun in time to catch Eva's attack. She managed three thrusts, but he was too fast – she hit nothing but air. Finally, he knocked her sword away and she was left with her dagger.

Kaeden shook his head. "Really? And how do you think that's going to turn out for you?"

Eva hurled the knife with unbelievable speed. Kaeden dodged right and back, but not fast enough. The knife sliced across the top of his shoulder, slicing it open and then sinking in the chest of a goblin standing behind him.

Kaeden snarled at the wound, his hand coming away bloody.

There was a lull in the battle, and I thought his werewolves might circle around their lord. Even though it was no more than a scratch, the dagger had been a few inches away from us winning the day.

But that wasn't the reason for the slow-down in the fight.

The real reason was that all of the Lesser Creach were either dead or had surrendered. Bodies covered the forest floor. A few werewolves appeared injured, but I couldn't see any fatalities. It hadn't been a fight – it'd been a slaughter. I searched for Skyal among the bodies but didn't see her. The demon had gotten away and taken my truthsayer with her. Something told me I might see them both again someday.

The wolves gathered around us in a circle, one by one converting to human form. They were of all ages, the youngest appearing to be in his early teens, all the way up to old men with grey beards and wise eyes. They looked back and forth between Eva and the blood on Kaeden's shoulder, not quite believing what they saw.

The four of us stood back-to-back, but it was

hopeless. There were too many of them. We might take a few with us, but no way were we going to win.

Eva was on my right shoulder. I spoke that direction without taking my eyes off the men in front of me.

"Why didn't you tell me?" I asked. "You let me believe you were a traitor."

"I knew they would use the truthsayer on you," she said. "If I told you the plan, you wouldn't have passed."

"The things I said to you. About your family... I'm sorry."

"Yeah, well, none of that's about to matter, is it?" she said.

Kaeden accepted a golden sword from one of his men. Intricate lettering covered the blade, and the hilt was encrusted with rubies, sapphires and diamonds.

"No vampire is allowed on my land," Kaeden said, speaking more to his men than to us. "And no boy is going to take the Jerusalem Stone that is mine alone by right."

He approached us, his face twisted with anger and filled with murderous intention.

This was one of the paths the Oracle had foreseen. If that dream was real, I should know what I had to do. I just couldn't remember her words..

I had to stall. "Kaeden," I yelled. "Stop."

To my surprise, he actually stopped.

I strained to remember what the Oracle told me. Kaeden growled and lifted his golden blade. At that moment, a narrow shaft of sunlight shone through the dense trees and lit a ruby on the sword's hilt. The reflection hit me square in the eyes. That did it. The Oracle's words shot back into my mind.

Now that I knew, I didn't want to repeat her words. They were a death sentence.

Kaeden lunged, snarling.

I jumped aside, but the sword took a piece of my sleeve. I had to talk fast. "As ones who drew your blood in battle, we demand a trial of honor." At least the Oracle's words would delay my death. .

A murmur rose among the men, several of them nodding their heads in agreement. Kaeden stared me down, shaking with suppressed anger. "What do you know of our ways?" he asked.

"I know that this request must be fulfilled. That all in our group must be held together and tried together," I said.

"You mean condemned together," he spat. "And you others, do you ask for the same? Do you ask for a trial of honor?"

Knowing that whatever it was, the trial was better than the certain death we faced in the forest, the others agreed.

"Yes," Daniel said.

"Sure, you bet," Will added.

Eva didn't respond. I turned to her. "It's our only chance," I said. "You drew his blood so you have to agree."

Eva finally looked up at me. "Do you know what this means? Do you know what we have to do?"

I nodded. "It'll buy us time," I whispered. "Give us a chance to find another way. Xavier and T-Rex are still out there somewhere. They can help us."

"There's no way we survive the trial," Eva said. "My vampire blood, it gives me memories of past lives. I can see what we will face."

"But there's no way we survive these werewolves right now," I said. "I don't see another way out."

"What's your decision?" Kaeden asked.

"Come on, Eva," I said. "It's the only way."

She nodded. "I also demand a trial of honor."

Kaeden turned and strode away. "Put them in the cage. They come with us."

The men closed in, took our weapons, and shoved us toward the cage.

"What did we just get ourselves into?" Daniel asked.

I hesitated to tell him, but I knew I had to. "It's a trial by battle."

"Who do we battle?" Will asked. "Kaeden?"

"No," I said. "Something a little harder than that."

"Who could be harder than that?" Will asked.

"The Oracle told me about it and how the werewolves of the Black Forest are tied to it," I said.

"What are you talking about?" Daniel nearly shouted.

"Oy, shuddup," one of the men growled.

Our escorts threw us roughly into the cage, and we ended up in a tangle of bodies. After we separated ourselves and each took our own space in the cage, I looked at them in turn.

"Sorry, guys, but it was the only way out I could see," I said.

"You're not talking about what I think you're talking about, are you?" Daniel said. "Because if you are, it's... well... impossible."

Will looked completely confused. "If you don't tell me what's going on, I'm going to punch someone in the nose."

With a lurch, the wagon started forward, bumping over the body parts of the goblins slain by the werewolves.

"Jack agreed to have us face one of most powerful creatures in the world," Eva said. "If we want to get out of here alive, we're going to fight and defeat the Boros."

Chapter Twenty-Three

"I thought you said the Boros didn't really exist," Will said, looking at Daniel for confirmation.

"It doesn't," Daniel said. "I mean, it can't really, right?"

"Oh, it exists," Eva said with a confidence that made us all turn her direction.

"You know something, don't you?" Daniel asked.

Eva shrugged. "One of the *benefits,*" she said, making the word sound like a curse, "of being injected with the blood of an ancient vampire, is that it comes with a certain amount of knowledge."

"Then what do you know about it?" Will asked.

A werewolf jumped at the cage, teeth bared and snarling. "Silence!" it growled. The wolf face contorted in ways I didn't think possible as it formed words and spoke as a human. "Next one who speaks, I chew off someone's leg. And I'm hungry. Understand?"

Will opened his mouth to answer, but I kicked him hard. He shut his mouth and drew his legs up toward him.

The wolf took up a loping stride right next to our cage, eyeing us with uncomfortably ravenous looks. We rode the next few hours in silence.

Over time, the open pines gave way to an old growth forest of gnarled oaks and tall, creaking birch. Although the sun had peaked only an hour or two before, the woods here were dark and ominous, overgrown with vines and briar bushes. Our werewolf escorts moved silently through the thick underbrush, making me think there must be secret passages and links throughout. Eventually, the wagon stopped when it came to a twenty-foot-high wall of thorny bushes. We were ordered out and each paired up with a werewolf. Walking single file, we entered the thicket through an opening barely wide enough to allow the wolves to pass.

I watched Daniel carefully, knowing how agitated he was to be around the same Creach who'd killed his father and brothers. He was tense, but then again we all were. Most important, he seemed in control. I think without his experience with Tiberon at the Academy, he wouldn't have been able to hold back. We would have found ourselves in a brutal battle to the death with these werewolves, right in the middle of the thorn bushes. And it wouldn't have ended well.

As we walked farther along, I realized the bramble patch didn't just seem like a maze, but most definitely was one. It twisted and turned. Offshoots headed off in different directions, some overgrown with weeds, others well worn. I had an idea that the well-worn trails were just as likely to lead to dead-ends as those covered with weeds. If an adventurous hiker decided to try to navigate the maze, he would likely find himself lost forever.

In answer to this thought, we passed by a human skeleton lying on the side of the path, curled up in a ball. I shivered as we passed, imagining T-Rex or Xavier getting lost in the maze if they tried to follow us. I was glad I'd been carefully digging my heel into the ground at each turn to leave a mark. I didn't know if it would be enough, but at least it was something.

I heard Will gasp ahead of me, so I craned my neck to one side to see what was going on. The maze opened onto a clearing in front of a sheer rock face of dark granite. Between the shadows, the creeper vines, and the scrub brush that clung to the rock, it looked like just plain rock at first. But as I looked closer, I could see why Will had gasped.

An entire castle was cut directly into the solid rock. High walls, parapets, arched windows, stations for archers; it had everything a regular castle would have. Only this had some of its features still locked into solid stone with only an outline carved into the rock to fool the eye. The entire thing made my brain hurt as it tried to understand what it was seeing. If I didn't know better, I'd think the castle had frozen into the rock the way a stone might freeze in ice, half in and half out, locked up and unmovable without first thawing or crushing the ice. Nothing was going to thaw or crush this mountain though, so it truly was stuck there for eternity.

The werewolves headed for the main gate. As we drew closer, I noticed the mountain above leaned out over the face of the castle, creating a lip. A fortunate result of the work done eons ago to create the place, it served as a perfect protection against modern day surveillance monitors like aircraft and satellites. A bored fifth grader looking at Google Earth in the Black Forest would see a mountain face and nothing more. Between that and the natural barrier of the bramble maze, it was easy to see why Kaeden had been able to keep his hideout a secret. It also proved that Eva's risky plan to use me as bait to lure Kaeden out had been the only way we would have ever gotten close to him.

But she hadn't known that when she first turned me over to the Creach. For all she knew, they might have killed me on sight.

Still, it was hard to be angry with her, especially after the horrible things I'd said to her about leaving her family behind. I knew that particular wound was still open, and me lashing out at her was just about the worst thing I could have done to hurt her. And that's what I'd been trying to do – hurt her as much as I could because I thought she'd betrayed me. I kept learning Aquinas's truth over and over. We tended to hurt most those we loved. I resolved to make it up to Eva somehow or at least try to earn her forgiveness before this was all over. The challenge of getting her friendship back made the upcoming battle with the Boros seem easy by comparison.

We passed through the main gate. It reminded me of the gate that led to the Cave of Trials back at the Academy. The one I'd finally used to crush the dragons in the goblin battle. But while the walls there had been fortified with spikes and counter-measures, this place looked like a ruin, crumbling in places, the iron clasps in the stone rusted through. If someone were to stumble across this place, they would only think they'd found an amazing relic of the past. Then again, if they stumbled across this place, they didn't stand a chance of getting back out into the world to share the news.

But if enough humans came, using their modern machines to cut through the brambles and their flying aircraft to get better images of the castle, there would be no way to kill them all to keep it a secret. The fact that Kaeden allowed his keep to appear this way said a lot about him. He was unwilling to relocate somewhere more remote, but he was a realist. It appeared that he knew discovery was a real possibility living in the middle of Western Europe in the twenty-first century.

My eye caught on the interior of the battlements where newer stone mixed with the old. Here, the iron was well oiled and weapons stood at the ready. The image of the castle as an old ruin was for show.

The werewolves wouldn't give up their keep easily if an army of other Creach arrived at their outer walls.

We passed through a cavernous hall lined with columns every bit as impressive as the inside of Notre Dame Cathedral. The air was stale and lifeless. Creeper vines covered the walls, covering murals of faded colors, twisting around the columns like angry fingers trying to tear them down. There were gouges in the rock walls, and some of the pillars had large cracks running through them. This hall had seen its share of battles.

In evidence of this, piles of rusting suits of armor lay heaped along the edges of the hall. They were battered, scarred black with flames, or punctured with gaping holes. I realized these were the Knights of the Teutons in the Oracle's prophecy. This place must have once been theirs until taken in battle by Kaeden, the armor left to rust as testament of their defeat.

At the far end, a throne made of black granite rose up from the floor, a reminder that this entire place had been carved out of solid rock. The time and effort it must have taken were staggering to consider.

Kaeden was already there, sitting on the throne in human form, his right hand resting on a human skull.

"You are the first humans to be allowed in these walls for centuries," he said, his voice echoing through the hall. The sound made the place seem somehow even more empty and abandoned. He nodded at Eva. "For your kind, it has been even longer. But I sense old blood in you. Maybe you have a memory of how this place once was?"

I turned to look at Eva who turned in a slow circle, taking in the surroundings. She closed her eyes and smiled. "It was wonderful," she whispered. "Filled with light and beauty." She opened her eyes and frowned at the dark ruins around her.

I shared a look with Daniel and Will. I got the sense that none of us liked seeing evidence of Eva's strange powers or the memories stored within her vampiric blood. It made her seem even more detached from her human self. It made her seem more lost to us.

For Kaeden, it had the opposite effect. He looked at Eva with new interest. He stood and strode to her, looking her over. He took one of her hands and held it to his mouth. I struggled forward, thinking he intended to hurt her. The guard behind me grabbed me by the collar and yanked me backward painfully.

But the Lord of the Werewolves didn't hurt her. He simply placed his nose to her wrist and took a deep breath, pulling in the smell of her.

He leaned back and sighed. "Ahh, I thought I smelled something familiar. Something I've not been near for centuries. You have the blood of Vitus in you."

I heard the venom in his voice when he said the name, and I feared that he might lash out at Eva from the anger there. Vitus. I knew the name from the story Shakra told me from her childhood, back when she was known only as Caroline, the daughter of a French noble at the first turning of the millennia.

Back before she needed the taste of blood to live.

The story was about the night she and my mother became vampires. How my grandfather, Ren Lucre, had lured the ancient vampire called Vitus to his castle, meaning to take his powers. Instead, Vitus had turned on Ren Lucre, forcing him to become a vampire, sealing the fate of my mother and her twin sister to be vampires as well. But Vitus's treachery was his last as the little girls, my mother and her sister, surprised the old vampire in an attack that ended his reign.

By the sound of Kaeden's scorn for the name, I guessed he also had a history with the old vampire.

"Vitus did not create me," Eva said carefully, as if sensing that one wrong word or the wrong tone could mean death. "Shakra did, Lord of the Vampires, daughter of Ren Lucre, the one who killed Vitus after he gave the gift to ¬¬–"

Kaeden's face half-transformed into that of a werewolf, a grotesque mask of hatred. "You call these curses *gifts*. Look around you. Nothing but ruin and desolation. Those are the only *gifts* these dark powers bring."

Most creatures in the natural world would have bowed their heads in submission in the face of such fury, but not Eva. She stared right into Kaeden's monstrous face without expression, like a stone in a storm, immovable. He stood in front of her, chest heaving, his face slowly turning human again as he regained control.

"I meant no offense. That is the word used in the memories given to me with this blood," Eva said, adopting the overly formal tone that he used. "Do you think I find this to be a gift? I was made a vampire without my consent. I ache with hunger because I refuse to feed. I walk on the brink of madness because of my despair over my betrayal." Her words hit me between the eyes and ripped my heart to shreds, but she didn't even glance at me as she continued. "This is no gift, Kaeden, Lord of the Werewolves. Of that, I am sure." Eva slowly looked down to Kaeden's feet and then back up to his face, sizing him up. "So, if you're done with your temper tantrum, let's discuss the Boros and how we are to defeat it."

We all held our breaths. I felt the presence of the werewolf guards draw closer in behind us. It was a risky move – insulting a Lord always is. I wondered if Kaeden might decide he'd had enough and give the order to have our throats ripped out so he could go back to sitting on his lonely throne in his ruined castle. Or he might throw us in whatever dark dungeon this place had and let us waste away for a decade or two. Of all the possible reactions, the one he chose surprised me most. He laughed in short barks.

"Temper tantrum," he said under his breath, clearly amused by the sound of the words. He turned his back on us and walked back to his throne. "I told you earlier that you are either brave or reckless. I'm still not certain which is the case." He sat and faced us. "That goes for all of you."

I stepped forward. "Sire, I don't know which of those two things we are, but I do know that we are committed to our quest."

"To steal my Jerusalem Stone," Kaeden said, the edge returning to his voice. His hand drifted up the spot on the armor breastplate encasing the stone.

"No, to stop Ren Lucre. To keep him from starting the war he wants between Creach and humans."

"Ren Lucre is a fool," the werewolf spat.

"There's the saying, my Lord," Daniel said. "That the enemy of my enemy is my friend. I know there is no love between vampires and werewolves. Perhaps –"

"And what do you know of the relationship between vampire and werewolf?" Kaeden sneered.

"He was a big *Twilight* fan," Will said.

Kaeden furrowed his brow and looked confused. I elbowed Will in the ribs.

"Everyone knows of the hatred between our two races," Eva said. "Even the Black Guard's history books are filled with the werewolf victories over the vampire hordes."

I suppressed a grin and felt a little of my tension release. I liked the new sound of confidence and control coming from Eva. I just hoped she didn't end up going too far.

Kaeden shook his head. "I forget what it's like to be human. To think of only a few generations as history. No, it was not always this way. It was not until Ren Lucre that things changed forever."

And then Kaeden, Lord of the Werewolves, told us a story that no human might have ever heard before. I stood there, fascinated, caught up in the intrigue and mystery of it all, but with a terrible thought brewing in the back of my mind. I realized the only reason he told us the story was because he didn't expect any of us to live through the night.

Chapter Twenty-Four

"I was born in Rome at the height of the Republic," Kaeden said. "Rome was not only a city, it was an idea. A civilizing force that spread across the world, touching all of Europe, northern Africa, and the Middle East. Think of it; most of Europe lived in mud huts and barely scraped by while Rome bustled with a million citizens going to the theater, eating at restaurants, attending universities, and debating the great questions of the day in public buildings."

My head spun at the idea that I was speaking to someone who had actually been in ancient Rome, a place I knew only through history books. He was talking about a time nearly two thousand years ago.

"I was born to a wealthy family. Our kind were called patricians, which was just a nice way of saying we were the privileged few who lived off the work of others. Mine was an old family, able to trace its roots back to Rome's founding. My parents lived like royalty, and I, as their only child, was treated like a prince."

Kaeden's eyes took on a distant look, and I expected he was deep into his memories now, reliving parts of his past as he told his tale.

"I would like to say I was a good human for the few years when I was one of you, but that would be a lie," he continued. "Maybe I was destined to be mean and cruel, spoiled the way I was. Servants to do anything I asked. No consequences for any bad behavior. Never required to do anything I didn't want to do."

"Sounds like you were a spoiled brat," Eva said.

I flinched but Kaeden smiled at her.

"Spoiled. Yes, that is the right word for it. Like a piece of fruit left in the sun, I became something soft and rotten. And the smell of my wretched self attracted a pest," Kaeden said. "He was a young man, my same age and from one of the other old families of Rome. We traveled in the same circles, attended the same parties, behaved badly at the same taverns, but he always kept his distance from me. I thought nothing of it. Back then, all I cared about was my own good time. But one day he came to me with an offer."

"He was a werewolf?" Daniel asked.

"No, he was human – if you can call someone so dark and mean-spirited human. But he was not of the Creach. Not yet. That was his offer."

"But if he wasn't a Creach, how could he make you one?" I asked. Kaeden shot me a dirty look. "Sorry," I mumbled. "Go on. Please."

"When he came to me, we were both nearing our seventeenth birthdays. Things were different then, and we felt that we were men, not boys. We actually felt like we were getting old. That our fun was coming to an end. So when he suggested we do something about it, I was an easy sell."

"He wanted you to find a way to become a Creach with him," Eva suggested.

I noticed Kaeden didn't mind interruptions from her like he did from Daniel and me. He gave her an approving smile that ticked me off. I wondered if I was going to have to get into a fight with the Lord of the Werewolves for trying to pick up the girl I liked. The idea was ridiculous, of course. Still, I ground my teeth seeing the way he looked at her.

"Yes, his proposal was that we combine our gold to fund an expedition to capture one of the mythological beings we'd heard about growing up. We called them gods back then, but they weren't any more gods than you and I are now," he said to Eva. "Do you think of yourself as a god?"

She shook her head. "More of a devil."

Kaeden laughed, annoyingly charming. "Exactly. But back then, we didn't know anything. We were just boys going off to chase fairy tales. We packed as much wine as we did weapons for our expedition. I thought it was all in fun, but my new friend was deadly serious. While I wanted an adventure to break up the boredom of endless parties with the same people, my friend was after eternal life. I should have seen it then. He was consumed with it. Nothing was going to stop Vitus from getting what he wanted."

"Vitus?" I asked, shocked.

This time Kaeden did not seemed annoyed but pleased.

"Yes, Templar," he said. "I'm glad to see you know him. I know Eva will access to memory of him, but I hoped that Shakra might have told you something of him as well."

"What's he talking about?" Daniel whispered. "Told you what? Who's Vitus?"

Kaeden laughed. "He doesn't know?" He shook his head in mock disdain. "Is that any way to treat your companions? I would have thought you would have told them your connection with Ren Lucre."

"Don't worry," I said. "They know Ren Lucre is my grandfather. I just never told them the story of how Ren Lucre lured an old vampire to his home and ended up being turned into a vampire by him. That old vampire's name was Vitus."

Kaeden looked disappointed that he hadn't found a weak spot in our group. I think he relished the idea of being the one to tell my friends I was related to our worst enemy. The fact that he thought I wouldn't have told them made me realize he didn't understand true friendship. I wondered if I could use that weakness later. I filed it away as Kaeden continued.

"Yes, Vitus had allowed himself to become old and ugly by the time he stumbled across Ren Lucre. I say *allowed himself* because vampires can control their aging process completely. He could have looked the same as the day he became a vampire if he chose, but he decided to let himself become an old, bald man."

Kaeden ran a hand through his mane of long hair, and I thought I saw him shudder at the idea. For a second, I saw the spoiled brat, the Roman noble who wanted things his way. The handsome guy who loved nothing more than to find a mirror with himself in it.

"He must have had his reasons," Eva said.

"I hope you will never have such reasons," Kaeden said to her. "It would be a shame to allow such beauty to wither."

I cleared my throat, feeling a little ridiculous the second I did it. But I felt better when I saw that Daniel looked jealous too. Kaeden smirked at the two of us like we were all just teenage boys who all liked the same girl, and he knew he had the upper hand. I had to remind myself that only one of us was a two-thousand-year-old werewolf from ancient Rome.

"But back then, Vitus was young and handsome," Kaeden said. "Wealthy. Charming. Smart. And completely terrified of growing old. Much like your grandfather, he set out to discover ways to cheat death. To become something more than human."

"To become a monster," Eva said.

Kaeden nodded. "Yes, but one with eternal life.

That was the goal."

"You make it sound like this was all Vitus," Daniel said. "Like you were some innocent bystander."

Kaeden scowled and looked only at Eva when he answered.. "No, he began the quest, but I bought into his delusion. Together, we sent out emissaries. We poured our families' gold into the search, nearly bankrupting ourselves in the process. But in the end, we found what we wanted. In fact, we found more than we'd bargained for."

Kaeden grew silent for a full minute, and we all let the time stretch out. He was clearly gearing himself up to tell us this last part of his story. My scalp tingled and my skin turned to gooseflesh as a cold wind passed through the great hall, making the burning torches flutter. It creeped me out. I had a hunch some evil power was at work, a power that didn't like this story being told.

Finally, Kaeden rose. I thought that he might of sensed the same power and changed his mind, but one look and I could tell he was determined to finish the tale. With his jaw set, staring into the distance like it he was lost in a different time and place, he told us the rest of his story.

Chapter Twenty-Five

"There were stories being told in the Northern mountains, whispered over glasses of ale at taverns in the small towns, dark tales of a strange creature. Normally, the ravings of superstitious commoners would be ignored, but it was just the type of information Vitus and I were willing to pay gold to hear, so it made its way to us. Vitus was immediately excited and we set off to investigate. Just the two of us, without servants or guards, which made me very uneasy.

"We arrived at a small village of Appia, long since crushed to dust by the grinding wheels of time.

There we heard of missing children. Of dark shadows that appeared at dusk and moved like creatures without bodies. Of three-horned beasts with red skin and glowing red eyes. The more people we asked, the more versions we heard of the terror haunting that cursed place."

"What was it?" I asked.

"What were they," Kaeden corrected. "You see, we had sought out a single creature that could give us eternal life. Instead, we had stumbled onto the site of a truly historical occasion in Creach history. A meeting of the Council of Lords. The heads of all five Creach – werewolves, vampires, zombies, demons, and the last a collection of all the rest – goblins, harpies, bloodslugs and so on. The Lesser Creach."

"That's impossible," Daniel said. "Ren Lucre was the first to unite the Creach. It was the reason the Templars were born. That wasn't for well over a thousand years later."

Kaeden shot Daniel such a look of disgust that Daniel's face fell, almost looking ashamed of his comment.

"Imply again that I'm a liar, and it won't be the Boros that destroys you today, but my own hands around your neck. Am I clear?"

Daniel swallowed hard and nodded.

The werewolf sniffed and then closed his eyes, collecting his thoughts. "No, this was the first Conclave of the Lords. The threat of the Roman civilization was so great that they felt they had no choice. Rome had united the world of men. Given it roads, governments, and systems that connected it all together. They knew it must be stopped if the monsters were to remain strong. Rome had to fall.

"I know all this because I heard them speak with my own ears. I won't bore you with the details of how I was able to hear their meeting, how Vitus and I spent three days crawling on our stomachs through a cave-system, how we infiltrated the guards by covering ourselves with goblin blood, how many times we were almost discovered but some twist of fate saved us. It is enough to say we were there and we heard their plans."

"I don't get it," I said, feeling stupid that I'd missed something. "What was their plan?"

"To erase the threat, of course," Kaeden said. "They plotted nothing less than the fall of the Roman Empire. And within a few generations, they achieved their goal. The world spiraled into a dark age that lasted for centuries."

"Wait," Will said. "So you're saying that the Roman Empire was brought down by the Creach? I thought it was the barbarians. You know, Nero fiddling while Rome burned and all that."

I was impressed Will had remembered his history, but not too surprised. I remembered the same lesson from our World History class, but Kaeden shook his head.

"Almost all of man's history is wrong," Kaeden said. "You should know this by now. The Creach operate behind the scenes, moving things in the direction that suits them. Ren Lucre has become the master at it, getting ready for his final war."

I caught the bitterness in his voice that bordered

on hatred for Ren Lucre and tried to think of a way to use it to our advantage. But before I could say anything, he continued.

"Besides, it was not the Creach that ended Rome's glory," Kaeden said sadly. "It was me."

"You told them how to do it," Eva whispered. "That's how you got what you wanted."

"They wanted to amass an army and march on Rome," Kaeden explained. "No matter how many tree giants and rock ogres they fielded, the legions of Rome were an unstoppable force. Vitus and I knew this, and we saw that they were doomed to failure. I took heart in this because I loved Rome, but Vitus saw this as his chance.

"He strode into the middle of Conclave, pulling me along, and announced who we were. I thought they might kill us out of hand, and the Lord of the Demons nearly did, but in the end, they listened to what Vitus had to say. He explained how he would do it. How he would cause Rome to rot from the inside. How he would destroy everything that made Rome special. How he would destroy the Republic by putting a Creach dictator on the throne."

"Wait a minute," I said, thinking through my world history. "Are you saying that Julius Caesar was a Creach?"

"Of course. He was a werewolf, to be exact," Kaeden said with some pride.

"But Caesar was killed in the Senate," Will said. "Stabbed like twenty or thirty times."

"More than it takes to kill a man," Kaeden replied. "But necessary to kill a werewolf. By then, it didn't matter. All the Caesars after him were Creach monsters, leading Rome down the path to its destruction."

"And for your treason, you got what you wanted," Eva said, the disgust showing in her voice.

"Yes, the vampires and werewolves had ancient hatreds between them, so each side took one of us for their own. After the transformation, Vitus and I worked together for centuries, protecting our own, pushing back the rise of man when necessary. All was good until Ren Lucre killed my friend. Because of him, vampires and werewolves have been mortal enemies ever since."

I wanted to tell him that my mother actually killed the old vampire, but I held back. I needed him to keep hating Ren Lucre.

"Then help me defeat him," I said. "Help me take the fight to your enemy."

Kaeden laughed, but it was a dark, brooding sound with no joy in it. "The Jerusalem Stones are a power you can't begin to understand. I was the one who insisted they be spread among the Five Lords for safekeeping after the defeat of the Templars. Why would I ever entrust them to a mere boy? A Templar, no less?"

"Because you know Ren Lucre's war will be a disaster," I said. "Just like you knew all-out war against Rome would be."

Kaeden shook his head. "Ren Lucre has his Creach everywhere. In governments. In the military. When the war comes, the President of the United States will give the order to attack, and half his army will turn on him and fire in the other direction."

"Surely you can see now that what you did with Rome was wrong," I said. "Mankind didn't just step backward, it plunged backward. We went from building the Coliseum and writing poetry to the Dark Ages of savage living and ignorance. Think of what man could have accomplished if we hadn't lost a thousand years of progress. Can you imagine where we could be now?"

Kaeden's expression softened, and I felt a surge of hope that I might have a chance reasoning with him.

"I don't want the Jerusalem Stones to conquer the Creach," I said. "Only to stop Ren Lucre's war."

"And free your father?" Kaeden asked.

The question caught me off-guard. I didn't imagine he would know about that. I could see he was evaluating me.

"If it came down to it and you had to choose between saving him and stopping Ren Lucre, which would it be?" he asked.

"I would find a way to do both," I replied. "Just like I would find a way to stop him and still find security for the Creach that want it in the human world."

"Bah!" Kaeden spat. "That is a fool's answer. He who tries to have it all ends up with nothing."

"He who never tries never fails but also never succeeds," Eva countered. "Not trying, just to avoid failure, that is the coward's answer."

Coming from her, it hit Kaeden like a slap on the cheek.

“Help us,” I pleaded. “Don’t let Ren Lucre make the same mistake the Creach Lords wanted to make almost two thousand years ago and start a war in the open. People have so much good in them. Who knows where the world might have been by now if Rome hadn’t fallen. Give humans a chance. They deserve it from you.”

Oops.

And I was doing so well before that last sentence. As soon as it crossed my lips, I had an idea it might be a mistake. It was.

“Deserve,” Kaeden sneered. “What do they deserve? Man has become a disease, rotting out everything that was once clean and pure. The air, the oceans, the soil, all contaminated amid this so-called progress. The Creach cower in shadows, forced into living as myths and ghost stories just to survive. Deserve!” He spit in the floor at my feet. “If I gave them what they deserve, they would already be dead.”

“I’m sorry,” I stammered, “What I should have said was ¬¬–”

“Enough!” Kaeden bellowed. “I’ve listened to this prattle for too long. You invoked the old ways, and so you will have your battle with the Boros. And you and your friends will meet your deaths at its feet.” He grinned at me. “If, by some mystery of fate, you survive, then you can have any one wish in my power to give you and safe passage from my lands. Let’s find out exactly what you deserve.” He waved a hand to his guards. “Lock them up. We call the Boros in an hour.”

The guards moved and manhandled us away from the throne toward a side door. I struggled against them, feeling my chance to convert Kaeden slipping away.

"You're making a mistake, Kaeden," I yelled.

"No, you made the mistake by bringing your companions here. And now they will all die because of it. Live with that, Jack Templar."

As the guards forced us through the doorway and into the dark passage deeper into the mountain fortress, a pit formed in my stomach. I realized Kaeden, Lord of the Werewolves, might be right.

Chapter Twenty-Six

We sat in our dingy prison cell, a torch with a small, smoky flame the only light in the room. By my estimation, we only had ten minutes or so left of our hour-long wait promised by Kaeden. So far, we really didn't have a strategy.

"Okay," Will said. "Let's go through it again to see if we missed anything."

Daniel groaned. "Saying the same things over and over isn't going to do anything for us. We need a plan."

I ignored Daniel's comment, mostly because it was about the fifth time he'd said it without actually coming up with any ideas.

"So the Boros is a Lesser Creach, but only in name. It's supposed to be an unstoppable armor-plated beast that fights dirty, moves quick as lightning, has teeth the size of my leg, and likes to eat its victims whole," I said.

"See, that's helpful," Daniel muttered.

"Maybe we could feed you to the Boros so it could choke on the taste of you?" Will said. "You are smelling a little ripe with no shower for the last couple of days."

Daniel didn't laugh. This was hard on all of us, but I knew being around werewolves was harder for him than for most because of his father and brothers.

"I hope T-Rex and Xavier are smart enough to stay away from this place," I said.

"Except that they're our last trick to play," Daniel said. "If they can somehow get past the defenses using Xavier's bag of tricks, they might give us a chance."

"From what I'm hearing, it would only add to this Boros thing's dinner menu," Will said.

"What do think, Eva? Any ideas how to beat this thing?" I asked.

She had stayed huddled in the corner since we'd gotten there and hadn't said much. When she looked up at me, I saw a strange fear in her eyes.

"I can see the Boros if I try," she whispered. "I know I should do it, but I can't bring myself to... to... go there."

I crouched down on the cold stone floor next to her. She was trembling. "What is it? What's going on?" I asked softly.

Eva put a hand on either side of her head as if she had a terrible headache and rocked back and forth. "I have all of their memories in here," she said. "All of Shakra's, all of Ren Lucre's, all of Vitus's. Sometimes images bubble up to the surface. Things that I couldn't possibly know except through them. When Kaeden told his story, I saw the cave where he and Vitus met the Lords. I could hear him speak."

I put my hand on her arm and was surprised to find her skin hot, almost feverish. Daniel and Will came closer, careful not to crowd her, but craning to hear what she said.

"They must have seen the Boros at some point, right?" Eva said. "So if I go into those memories, then I can find it. See if I can find a weakness."

"But it scares you," I said.

She nodded and drew in a shuddering breath. "I think all of their victims are in there too. When vampires feed, they're not drinking blood; they're drinking life. All the memories, the triumphs and failures, the joy and sadness. They consume a soul." She wrapped her arms across her chest, hugging herself. "If I go looking into the memories, I'm going to see every one of those deaths all over again. I don't know if I can do that."

"It's okay. You don't have to do it," I said. "We'll find another way."

"No, I have to try. I know that," she said. She grabbed my arm painfully hard and looked up at me. "Just make sure I come out of it."

Without warning, her eyes fluttered backward,

and only the whites of her eyes showed. Her body sagged as if all of her bones had suddenly disintegrated, leaving only a sack of muscles, organs, and skin.

"Help me," I called.

Daniel and Will rushed forward, and we laid Eva flat on the floor. Her eyes remained open, but still rolled back, giving her a creepy look in the torchlight. No, it would have been creepy even in the full light of day.

Her body began to twitch, and small whimpers came from her open mouth. She reminded me of someone having a bad dream, except I knew she was seeing actual memories of the ancient vampires whose blood filled her veins.

Her legs kicked out straight and her body went stiff. Her mouth opened in a soundless scream.

"That's enough," I said, shaking her. "Wake up. Eva. Come on. Wake up."

Her legs kicked as if something was attacking her. Her arms flailed. She found her voice and screamed, "NO!"

"Eva!" I cried. I looked to Daniel and Will. "What do we do?"

They both looked terrified.

"I don't know," Daniel said.

I took her by the arms and shook her. Gently at first, and then harder and harder. "Eva. Wake up. It's Jack. I'm right here. Eva!"

Then she was back. Her eyes rolled down into place, and her body relaxed. She sat up and stared at the flame on the wall as if the light would chase away the darkness where she'd just been.

"Was it as bad as you thought?" I asked.

"No," she said. "It was worse than I could have imagined."

The iron door to the prison cell rattled open.

"On your feet, vermin," the guard yelled. "You four have a date with the Boros to keep. Single file line. No talking."

Eva stood, and we all did the same, but I kept my eyes on her. "Did you learn anything?"

"You there," the guard barked. "You hear what I said? No talking."

Eva nodded and turned to me with a slight smile. "Yes, I think I did."

The guards pushed us forward down a long, wide tunnel carved into the rock. A few of them dropped down into werewolf form as we walked. They separated us, forming a long line with werewolves between each human so I wasn't able to get anything else from her. All I could do was follow the werewolf in front of me and hope that whatever Eva had discovered was going to be enough to get us through the upcoming fight.

I like to consider myself an optimist, but I have to admit, I didn't feel good about what was about to happen. I had every reason to be scared because there was nothing good waiting for us at the end of the tunnel.

Chapter Twenty-Seven

We entered an enormous circular pit with a sandy floor and walls of black granite extending twenty feet straight up before widening into dozens of rows of cut-stone seats for spectators. The cavern rose at least a hundred feet from the floor, and massive stalactites that looked like giant canine teeth covered the ceiling. Only the first couple of rows around the arena were filled, reinforcing the sense I'd gotten since coming here that this place and this group of werewolves had seen better days.

Kaeden stood in his human form on a rock platform that bowed out into the arena. In front of him lay a pile of weapons. Swords, spears, axes. I recognized the weapons the werewolves had confiscated from us among the others.

Seeing him there, I realized what this place was. It was a copy of the great Coliseum of Rome carved into the solid rock of the mountain. Kaeden played the role of Caesar overlooking the games, and we were the gladiators sent out to entertain the masses with our deaths. It wasn't a role I looked forward to playing.

"Jack, look," Will hissed.

He pointed to the sand in front of me. I hadn't noticed the white sticks half-buried in the sand when we first came in. Now that I saw the ones nearest me, I realized these white sticks were visible around the entire arena floor. I didn't think much of them, just filing it away in my mind as something to look out for in the battle ahead.

Will must have not been satisfied with my reaction because he walked up to the nearest stick and kicked it with the toe of his shoe. The sand fell away, and I saw that it was part of a rib cage half-buried in the sand. I turned and saw Eva nudge something with the bottom of her foot. The object rolled forward. It was a human skull, sand pouring from its eye sockets and its gaping mouth.

The white things weren't sticks. They were bones. Hundreds and hundreds of them. And that was only the top layer. As far as I knew, the bone pile might have been thirty feet or three feet deep. There was no way to tell.

What I could tell was that the werewolves had

played this game here for centuries and, based on the amount of bones, they were likely not very worried about us winning against the Boros.

I scanned the werewolf faces around the arena edge, mostly in animal form, some choosing to appear as humans. They stared at us with all the excitement of a crowd watching fish about to be shot in a barrel. They clearly did not expect this to be a very entertaining fight. I hoped they were wrong.

"Any sign of them?" Daniel whispered.

Before he asked, I didn't realize why I'd been searching the crowd – I was looking for T Rex and Xavier. I felt a weird mix of relief and disappointment that they were nowhere to be seen. I half-expected some kind of sign left for us to know they were there and waiting for the right moment to help. But I found nothing. They were safely outside the Keep's walls where they should be.

"Eva," I said. "Were you able to see anything in your memories? Anything that might help? Like how Kaeden and the Boros are linked?" I should have asked as soon as we stepped into the arena, but my brain was overloaded.

Eva's eyes scanned the sand surface. I thought the sight of the bones had gotten to her, maybe reminded her of the catacombs in Paris with its millions of dead inhabitants. But when she looked up, she looked neither panicked nor scared.

"I don't know the connection," she said. "No vampire witnessed that. But I know how it attacks. It'll come from under us. Up from the sand."

The three of us backed up, watching the surface

of the sand more carefully.

"Is it as bad as the stories?" Will asked.

"No," Eva said. "It's worse."

"Brothers and sisters," Kaeden intoned, holding his arms wide. "We gather to bear witness to a challenge. This vampire..." He paused as the spectators broke out of their eerie quiet with a sudden eruption of howls and snarls. Kaeden smiled at the reaction, clearly pleased by it. "This vampire is newly made but carries the blood of our ancient enemy, Ren Lucre."

This time the growls were twice as loud and angry. Kaeden waved his arms to get the others to fall silent.

"And these humans, who call themselves members of the Black Guard, one of them with Templar blood in his veins, wish to try their luck against the beast of the mountain, the Boros."

Kaeden pushed the pile of our weapons forward with his foot until it tipped over the edge of the rock promontory and fell the twenty feet to the sandy floor below. The werewolves erupted in a frenzy, snapping the air with their fangs, scratching their claws against the rock where they stood.

"He makes us sound like we wanted to do this," Will grumbled. "Last I checked, it was this or be killed back in the forest."

"It's part of the theatrics. Either way, we're here," Daniel said. "Come on, let's get our weapons and make a fight of it."

He took a step forward, but Eva shouted at him, "Wait! Don't move." She turned an ear toward the center of the arena and listened, head tilted.

"What is it?" I whispered.

She pointed toward the sand out in middle of the floor.

"It's already here," she said. "And it's hungry."

Chapter Twenty-Eight

We hung back, staring at the floor of the arena, searching for any indication of where the Boros might be hiding. I glanced back at the entrance to the tunnel we'd used to enter the pit to size up whether escape in that direction was possible if we needed it. A heavy metal gate had slide into place behind us.

"How do you know?" I whispered to Eva.

"Can't you feel the vibrations?" she asked. "Or smell it?" She held a hand to her mouth, looking nauseated from some kind of stench.

I drew in a long breath of air through my nose. There was the dampness from the cave, the gritty smell of the sandy floor, and the not-so-pleasant smell of my own clothes after two days without a shower. But nothing that would have warned me of a giant monster nearby.

I looked to Daniel and Will. They seemed just as puzzled. Eva's heightened vampiric senses were at work, and I realized they might be the edge we needed to be successful.

"We need to get our weapons," Daniel hissed.

The stretch of bone-filled sand was about the length of two basketball courts. That may not seem like much, but when your vampire friend tells you there is a giant monster lying in wait under the sand to devour you, it starts to look like a long distance run.

"Eva, we can't feel it or smell it," I told her. "You're our eyes and ears. Can we make it to the weapons?"

Her eyes darted back and forth, as if she was seeing something I couldn't. Then even I spotted tiny ripples in the floor. A bulge of sand. A bone fragment twitched from something moving beneath it.

"It's massive," Eva whispered.

"We can't very well just wait here for it to come get us," Will declared. "I'll draw it this way. You guys go for the weapons."

"Will, no!" I cried.

But it was too late. Once a thought entered Will's mind, it was usually only a matter of seconds before he acted on it. That impulsiveness had gotten him into a lot of trouble over the years but probably saved his life on more than one occasion. I was sure running off to attract the attention of the Boros by himself was in the trouble category.

"Hey, Boros!" Will shouted as he ran along the base of the circular wall to our left. "Over here!"

"Come on," Daniel said. "We can't help the crazy bugger when the Boros comes if we don't have our weapons."

He was right. We turned and sprinted to our right, working our way the opposite direction around the circle. A few seconds later, Eva whisked past us as if we were standing still, her vampiric powers making her two to three times faster than either Daniel or me. She reached the stack of weapons when we were still halfway around the edge. She didn't even break stride. Running at full speed, she bent down, grabbed two swords and a shield from the pile, and continued around the outer circle. Right toward Will.

Before she could reach him, and just before we reached the weapons, the Boros attacked.

The monster burst from the ground with such fury, sand and bones exploded into the air. The force of it blew me off my feet and threw me hard against the rock wall. Daniel hit the wall next to me and crumpled to the ground with a grunt.

A high-pitched shriek filled the air, so loud that I had to cover my ears from the pain. After the first burst of sound, it changed into a lower register and became a roar like from a lion or tiger. Well, maybe from a few dozen lions or tigers. I felt the roar in my chest in a low vibration that I thought might shake the bones right out of my body. At least it wasn't the piercing scream that felt like it would shred my eardrum.

I crawled to my knees and tried to get a look at the creature. At first, the cloud of sand and bones made it impossible to see. Dust hung in the air, a giant shadow in the center of the arena. But as this cleared, terrifying details of our adversary came into few.

The Boros was a mash-up of several creatures all in one body. It stood on thick hind legs, like a dinosaur's, and reared back, clawing the air with smaller arms that had wicked, barbed claws on the end. An armor-plated tail with spikes on it extended behind, thumping on the sand as the Creach moved.

Dark red scales covered the heavy body, glistening in the light from dozens of torches around the arena. Two sets of leathery wings stretched out from its spine and spread in the air like an insect flaring its wings. All of that sounds like I'm describing a dragon, but trust me, this was no dragon.

First, there was the head. While everything about the body suggested some kind of serpent or dragon, the Boros's head was a complete surprise. It looked like an enormous bull with bulging eyes, a snout with flaring nostrils hanging with long strands of thick mucus, and black, curved horns. As if that wasn't bad enough, I realized it was just the first head.

The Boros's second head had been hidden behind the first, and I didn't see it until it leaned back and let out a blood-curdling howl. This head was even more bizarre. Covered with coarse black fur, it had forward-facing beady eyes that glowed yellow. It had a long, fang-filled snout that would have made it look like a wolf except for the corkscrew horns on either side of its head where the ears ought to have been. I'm not sure which head, the bull or the wolf, was crazier looking. Bottom line, this thing was one ugly looking Creach.

"Jack, catch!" Daniel called.

Looking up, I saw my sword flying through the air toward me. I snatched it by the well-worn hit and sprang to my feet.

I didn't need to say anything to Daniel because he was already charging at the Boros with all his might.

As I ran toward it, the ground beneath my feet crunched from all of the bones brought up from the depths. I wondered how the beast was able to burrow through the earth, but I didn't have much time to think about it before the Creach tried to burrow one of the spikes on its tail through my chest.

I jumped just in time to avoid the worst of the tail, but I couldn't get high enough to clear it completely. It nicked my lower legs and spun me in the air. I landed headfirst, missing the scattered bones and falling on a clear patch of sand.

Daniel brought his sword down on the tail with a battle cry, but his weapon clanged off the armor and rebounded.

The bull-head spun around, eyes blazing. I heard a strange clicking noise as the Creach drew in a lungful of air, and I smelled charcoal in the air. It was a sound and smell I remembered well from the dragons.

"Daniel! Move!" I yelled.

We'd been in enough battles together that he didn't hesitate. He sprang forward, diving back over the tail just as a stream of fiery liquid burst from the bull's mouth. It splattered like gobs of mucus except that they were on fire.

The stuff covered the ground where Daniel had been standing, charring the bones in the sand. The wolf-head spun around to see what his partner in crime was up to. I hoped that would give Eva and Will a chance to break free.

But nothing moved on the opposite side of the Creach.

"Eva! Will!" I bellowed, fearing the worst had already happened. The Oracle's words came rushing back to me, the warning that all of us might die and the promise that no matter what, at least one of us would.

Finally, Eva and Will appeared on the far side of the Boros. The distraction had been enough to break them free. I saw that Will limped on one leg and Eva had to help him along. We already had one injury.

"You take the bull and I'll take the wolf head," Daniel shouted.

We charged forward, jumping over globs of burning goo, swords swinging. The Boros swiveled its enormous body toward us, both heads screaming at us. It came down hard on its arms so that it faced us on all fours, the heads now at our level instead of towering over us.

I swung my sword at the bull-head, aiming for one of its massive eyes. It dodged easily, much quicker than I expected for a monster this size. I ducked a swipe it made with its right arm and felt the air whoosh over the top of my head.

Next to me, Daniel made contact with the wolf-head, sinking his blade into a spot next to the Creach's nose. That head reared back, roaring. Not in any pain, but definitely angry.

"Watch out!" I cried. The Boros had arched its spiked tail over its own head like a scorpion. From his angle, Daniel couldn't see it, and he was about to get skewered.

In a blur of motion, Eva rushed up from behind us and pushed Daniel out of the way.

But she wasn't fast enough herself. The heavy tail smashed into her, knocking her head over heels across the arena. She smacked into the rock wall and sagged to the ground.

Even over the roaring Boros, I heard a cheer from the werewolf crowd gathered above us.

Both monster heads turned toward me. Stepping backward, I tried to draw the Creach away from my friends. I fended off a series of violent attacks, including another spray of fiery mucus.

I chanced a quick look over at Eva. She was moving, struggling to get back to her feet. The blow she took would have killed Daniel or me, but not her. I imagined her vampire blood rebuilding the tears in her skin and reforming her broken bones. It was happening slowly, so the damage must have been bad. I just hoped it didn't take too long because I didn't know how much longer I could hold off the Boros on my own.

I felt the cold steel of the gate where we had entered the arena against my back. The wolf-head howled, and the bull grunted in a slobber of molten fire. They had me and they knew it. With nowhere to run and no space to maneuver, there was no escape.

Then, just as the Boros reared back for its final, fatal strike, the craziest, most unexpected thing happened.

Chapter Twenty-Nine

The gate behind me slid open and I fell backward in a heap.

The Boros screamed in frustration as the gate closed, taking a full blast of the bull-head's fire. Then something smashed into the door, hard enough to dent it inward. A second blow added another dent, but the door held.

Hands grabbed at me and I struggled against them. I'd dropped my sword, so I went for the dagger at my waist.

"Jack, wait. It's just us."

I froze, and my eyes adjusted to the darkness in

the tunnel. I'd never seen a more beautiful sight as the two guys standing there.

T-Rex and Xavier.

"What... how did you...?" I stopped myself. They could have ridden in on the backs of a pack of mugwumps for all I cared. They were there and Xavier had his bag of tricks with him.

"We've got to get back in there," I shouted.

T-Rex looked scared to death, but he nodded. "Do you think we can beat that thing?" he asked.

I looked down and saw that he carried a mean-looking crossbow with one of Xavier's canisters screwed into the top of the bolt where the arrowhead would normally be. He shoved it into my hands.

"How powerful is the explosive on that bolt?" I asked.

Xavier shrugged. "I haven't had time to properly test –"

"Is it a big or a small explosion?" I shouted.

"Big," he replied. "Pretty big, I think."

Xavier dove into his backpack again, rummaged through it, and came up with new items. He held three small bags in his hand and gave me another arrow with a canister on top. He shook his head. "But I don't think the arrows will be powerful enough. Its armor looks too thick."

"We've got to try," I said. "Open the door, T-Rex. Let's get into the fight."

T-Rex yanked on a pulley next to the door, and the mechanism cranked the door open, revealing the Boros in the center of the arena. Will attacked one side and Daniel the other. I spotted Eva stumbling toward the fight, not quite recovered.

T-Rex, Xavier, and I ran into the pit, yelling at the top of our lungs.

Xavier threw three bags at the Boros. When they burst open, clouds of smoke filled the air, giving us the extra cover we needed.

The Boros turned to face this new threat, both heads screeching angrily at sight of the prey that had gotten away.

Will and Daniel used the opportunity to press their attack, getting dangerously close.

Soon, we had the thing encircled, the six of us united again, ducking in and out of the cover provided by Xavier's smoke bombs.

The Boros lunged at whichever one of us was closer, the two heads sometimes going in opposite directions, yanking them both back with a snap.

We had it confused. It started to make bad decisions out of frustration, lunging too far forward and leaving itself open for a cut here, another blow there. I decided to go for broke.

"Heads up!" I yelled. "Everyone get back!"

Everyone turned and ran toward the outer walls. The Boros froze, then slowly turned toward me, realizing it was caught in a trap.

"Sorry, big guy," I said. "But this is what you get for messing with the Black Watch."

I took aim with the crossbow and let the bolt fly. It arced perfectly through the air and hit dead center in the massive Creach's chest.

The explosive detonated in a gigantic ball of

flame. A wave of heat blasted over me, and I dropped to the ground with my arms up to cover my face. It was way more powerful than I'd expected. Xavier was likely grinning from ear to ear.

I looked up, expecting to see the gruesome wreckage of the monster littering the arena. Instead, all I could see was the white smoke from Xavier's smoke bombs mixing and swirling with the black smoke from the explosion.

It all hung low in the arena like a fog over a swamp.

Everything was silent. Even the werewolf spectators stood hushed. I glanced up at the rock promontory where Kaeden remained motionless, his face caught in a wince of pain.

My confidence surged. Surely, Kaeden could see into the smoke from where he stood better than I could. I read the look of pain on his face as a sign that he'd been beaten. That he knew I was going to ask for the Jerusalem Stone as my one wish he was in a position to grant me.

But as I watched him, the wince disappeared and slowly but surely turned into a wicked grin.

With a roar, the Boros burst out from the smoke, beating its massive wings so the smoke blew out of the pit, up toward the roof of the cavern where it swirled among the giant stalactites. The werewolves howled in approval as the Boros rose to its full height and stretched out every claw and spike in a display of force.

It was completely unharmed.

My heart sank. If an explosion that size couldn't

hurt this thing, then what good were our puny swords and spears?

I woke up from my little pity party at the sound of Eva's battle cry ringing in my ears.

She was charging the Boros single-handed as the rest of us stood open mouthed. And she was right. What else was there to do, even in the face of impossible odds? Give up? Not likely.

That was our creed after all. *Do your duty, come what may.*

In this case, the *come what may* was a two-headed monster who could breathe fire and barely flinch when what amounted to a bomb exploded in its chest.

But the *duty* part hadn't changed. And if this was where we were all meant to face our end, then we would do it with honor.

I ran toward the Boros, crossbow tucked under my arm with the extra explosive arrow in my hand. Ridiculously, I pulled out my dagger while I ran, as if I was going to slay this beast with a blade hardly the length of my forearm. The explosive wasn't going to work either; I'd just seen that with my own eyes, so the dagger was no more ridiculous than any other weapon any of us were using. Besides, it felt fitting to go out with a blade in my hand.

Eva engaged the bull-head, dodging jets of fiery goo, getting in small cuts and stabs on the soft tissue around the mouth, but not really doing anything to hurt it.

Instead of taking positions about the monster like we had before, we clustered together this time.

It was as if we all subconsciously wanted to be together in the end, fighting shoulder to shoulder like we had so many times before.

I managed to slide the bolt into the crossbow and used the hand crank to arm it. I thought maybe if the Boros gave me a shot with its mouth open, then maybe that would be a way out for us. Even then, I was sure the other head would finish us off.

"Keep it up," Daniel yelled. "Fight to the end."

We all surged forward, giving everything we had. Eva moved like a blur. Xavier clumsily wielded a spear but did his best with it. T-Rex and Will stood so close together they looked like they had one body with two heads, just like the Boros.

"Watch it," I yelled as a jet of fire streaked their direction. At the last second, Will saw it and pushed T-Rex out of the way before jumping clear himself.

The image stuck with me, and a thought stirred deep in my mind. The way they were so close together. How the fire almost took them out at the same time. There was something there, I was sure of it. Only I couldn't....

As if in answer to me trying to think of a way out, the heads of the Boros screamed louder than anything I'd heard yet. I held my hands to my ears and the others did the same. A second too late, I realized it was a trap.

The Boros crouched low and spun in a circle faster than I thought possible given its size. Its armor-plated tail whipped along the sand covered floor and took all of us out in one mighty swipe.

Fortunately, none of us was hit square on like

Eva had been. All of us dodged just enough to avoid serious damage, but each one of us fell, sending our weapons scattering. Every weapon, that is, except the crossbow, and that had nothing to do with me holding it.

In fact, it was tangled in my shirt and just came along for the ride. I landed with it painfully jutting into my ribcage. It hurt, but that was a far cry better than the explosive tip going off, which it could very easily have done if I'd landed in a slightly different angle.

I rolled over onto my back, my ears still ringing from the Boros's roar. Looked to my left and right, I saw all my friends sprawled out on the ground around me, groaning. The Boros rose up on its rear legs in a triumphant pose.

The werewolf audience ate it up, howling and snarling with delight. The anticipated boring slaughter had ended up given them more fun and interest than they'd expected. Now it was time for the show to end.

The Boros looked to Kaeden, just like a gladiator in ancient Rome looking to Caesar, asking whether to give mercy to the opponent.

The werewolves fell silent, and I heard nothing but my ragged breathing and the thumping of my own heart in my ears. There was a long pause, and I felt a surge of hope that Kaeden would spare our lives.

"Would you like to know why the Boros serves me so faithfully?" he called. He must've wanted to stay in the spotlight a while longer.

"Sure," I croaked, aching all over. It couldn't hurt to get on his good side.

Kaeden nodded. "Long ago, the Teutonic Knights captured the Boros using the Templar Ring. And with it, they created a pit so deep and slippery, the Boros couldn't crawl out, so narrow, it couldn't fly out, and so hard that nothing could escape. Not even a creature used to tunneling through solid rock."

The Boros let out twin angry bellows, and I thought it was going to trample me right then. But Kaeden calmed it with a shake of his head before continuing.

"The Templars didn't count on me capturing their castle. When I found the pit, I fed the Boros for the first time in centuries – with all the captured Templars my warriors hadn't already eaten."

While the audience roared in delight, I felt my pain melt away as red hot anger filled me. Was the Boros smiling? Kaeden sure was. He swept an arm out and around the arena.

"As we excavated the ordinary rock above the original pit, the Boros itself crushed the debris into sand, slowly working its way upward to its new home. A showcase dedicated to its glory. As you can see by the bones, it's never gone hungry since."

I swallowed hard and glanced at my fallen friends. Only Eva was moving. "It doesn't have to be like this," I cried out. "I don't believe all monsters are evil, and if I can gather the Jerusalem Stones –"

Kaeden smiled and held out his hand, thumb held sideways. Maybe I'd gotten through to him. But that was exactly the false hope he wanted. Once our eyes met and he saw the flicker of anticipation in mine, he grinned and turned his thumb downward.

No mercy.

The werewolf crowd went crazy and both heads of the Boros roared.

I readied the crossbow for one last shot. We were all too close to it this time. The explosion wouldn't kill the Boros, but it would take all of us out, robbing the beast of the final kill.

I balanced the weapon in shaking hands and took aim.

The image of Will and T-Rex fighting right next to each other sprang into my head.

I flipped off the safety catch.

Something about how the fire stream nearly got them both at the same time.

At the same time.

With a yell, I rocked backward and fired the crossbow upward, far over the Boros. The bolt soared into the open air above the monster, and the Boros ignored it, marching toward us, claws outstretched.

It ignored the sound of the impact two seconds later high above in the ceiling.

It didn't react when the werewolves started to cry out in warnings.

In fact, it barely reacted when the hundred-ton stalactite dislodged from the cave ceiling by the explosive bolt crashed into its body from above, piercing it through like a giant spear.

Barely reacted, I say, because the dead find it hard to do more than lie there and bleed. Except for a few involuntary twitches, that was exactly what Boros did.

I stood up, slouched to one side, seeing the world at bizarre angle. I couldn't quite believe my eyes, so I didn't want to stand up straight at the risk of ruining the sight in case it was all just a beautiful optical illusion. If it was, I wanted to keep it in its place for as long as possible.

I glanced up at Kaeden and saw a horrified look on his face, one hand to his mouth and the other on the Jerusalem Stone embedded in his chest plate.

That look was enough for me.

I stood up straight, raised my fist in the air, and cheered. Tears sprang to my eyes, the stress of the battle finally overtaking me.

As I ran to Eva, she stood up. Daniel, Will, T-Rex, and Xavier managed to get their feet and clustered around us, hugging, crying, and sharing soft words that we were all okay.

"We made it, Jack," T-Rex said. "We all made it."

Will gripped my shoulder, grinning. "See?" He pointed to the stalactite sticking up in the air in the center of the ring, the Boros skewered beneath it. "The old Oracle didn't see that coming, did she? Must have changed the whole thing."

"Yeah," I replied, the excitement of victory fading into a rising sense of dread as I remembered the Oracle's warning that one of us would die. "I guess she was wrong."

I looked up to Kaeden who still stood alone on the promontory of rock. I didn't like the expression on this face. It wasn't an expression of defeat, only pure anger and hatred.

Without a sound, he leapt from his perch toward the arena floor. Halfway down, he converted from his human form into a werewolf. He bounded at us in five great leaps. With a snarl, he knocked Daniel over, viciously bit into his shoulder, and dragged him ten yards away from us.

Our battle wasn't over yet.

Chapter Thirty

"Kaeden, we had a bargain," I shouted. "Let him go."

Kaeden shifted back into his human form. He grabbed a dagger lying in the sand and held it to Daniel's throat. Daniel struggled, but Kaeden simply grinded the hilt of the dagger into the bite-wound until Daniel whimpered.

"Is that your wish of me, Templar?" Kaeden said. "For besting the Boros, I owe a debt of one wish within my power to grant. Is it the release of your friend that you wish?"

"Kill him, Jack," Daniel mumbled. "Told you... can't... trust a ¬¬–" He screamed in pain as Kaeden pressed against his wound again.

"We killed the Boros," Will said. "Where's your honor?"

Kaeden growled in a way that sounded like it could only have come from his werewolf self. "Speak to me of honor again, boy, and I'll tear out all your throats, old magic or not."

"You know I came here for the Jerusalem Stone," I said, searching for a way out of this mess. "I intend to leave with it, one way or the other."

Kaeden hefted Daniel up to his feet and pulled back his shirt, showing us the deep wound on Daniel's chest. It was deep, really deep, but it hardly bled. I didn't like the look of that at all.

"This is a very special kind of bite," Kaeden said. "But I can see on your face that you already know that. Am I right?"

I nodded. I had guessed before, but his words left me no doubt.

"This is the transforming bite. The one that will make him into a werewolf. But I can stop it from happening," Kaeden said. "It is within my power. Do you understand?"

I nodded. "It is a wish you are able grant for killing the Boros."

Kaeden grinned. "Exactly. It's said among the Creach that you care too much for the lives of your companions to ever defeat Ren Lucre. They see this as a great flaw. I, on the other hand, think this is your most admirable quality."

"You're just a lying dog," Will belted out. "You gave your word."

"And I have every intention of keeping it," Kaeden said.

Daniel's eyes rolled back so that only the whites showed. His body went stiff, and he began to shake. Kaeden continued to hold him up for us to see.

"What's wrong with him?" T-Rex asked.

"The curse is finding its way through his body," Kaeden growled. "It's not too late to reverse it, but soon it will be. A decision must be made." He pointed a long finger at my chest. "What is the thing you want from me, Templar? The Jerusalem Stone so you can chase the ridiculous fantasy of reuniting them once again? Or do you want to save your friend from becoming the one thing he most hates in the world?"

I looked at Daniel, my tears welling. I felt like I was back at the catacombs again, one of my friend's lives in the palm of my hand. It was too much responsibility for me to bear again.

I thought of what Daniel had told me when I wanted to abandon our quest to go look for Eva after Xavier told us she'd escaped from Aquinas's care. *When it's my turn, if there's a choice to make, I will sacrifice everything to this cause. It is simply that important.*

Something like that was easy to say before looking death in the face. It was a different matter now that it was real and right in front of us. I wondered if he would say the same thing now.

I looked to Will, T-Rex, and Xavier. All I saw in their faces was support for whatever decision I made. I saw their sympathy that another impossible situation had fallen on my shoulders.

Eva spoke up behind me. "You made the right decision," she said.

I turned and blinked hard, trying to understand. "But I haven't... I don't know what I should do...."

"I mean with me," she said softly. "You made the right decision, and I never thanked you for it. You knew how much I want to live. You were right; I cut off my own hand to escape Ren Lucre. Not to run, not to go find help, but to live."

"Eva, I didn't mean –"

"Thank you for the decision you made. Thank you for knowing me well enough to know what I would want even though it's taken me a while to understand it myself." She pointed to Daniel. "Do him the same honor. Make the decision that shows you truly know him as a friend. If you do that, you cannot do wrong."

"Enough of this," Kaeden said. "The time comes when this will not be reversible by anything less than the five Jerusalem Stones themselves. What is your answer? Save your friend or take the Jerusalem Stone?"

I looked at each of my friends once again, and they each nodded their encouragement. After what Eva had said, we all knew the answer to the question.

"I choose to save my friend," I cried, addressing both Kaeden and the assembled werewolves all around us. "...by keeping his honor intact. While he'll despise the way he'll have to live, being the reason we didn't acquire this Jerusalem Stone would be worse than death to him." I pointed to Kaeden's armor where the stone now glowed bright red. "Kaeden, Lord of the Werewolves, I demand as my tribute the Jerusalem Stone in your possession."

The stone tore from his armor and flew through the air. I caught it in my hand, expecting it to burn me since it glowed so brightly. But it didn't. It turned back to its normal color, a simple stone like any other river rock. I gripped it tightly, all too aware what it had cost.

Daniel legs buckled beneath him. He fell to the ground, panting. His arms stretched, and he cried out in pain. Hair sprang from his body. His face was the last thing to disappear, but for a split second his eyes met mine, and I saw in them a moment of clarity. He looked right at me and nodded in approval.

At least that was what I hoped I saw.

A few seconds later, Daniel's face was gone, replaced by a snout and fangs. We had the Jerusalem Stone, but the Oracle had been right. One of my friends had died. Daniel the human was no more. All that remained was Daniel the werewolf.

He arched his back, stretching to feel the full power of his new body. He flexed his claws and bared his teeth in a snarl. Finally, he leaned his head back and let out a mournful howl, so filled with sadness and regret. it brought tears to my eyes and made me doubt the look I saw on his face before he transformed.

"Daniel," I said. "If I made the wrong decision, I'm sorry." I held up the Jerusalem Stone so he could see it. "We have three more of these to find," I said. "And we could use your help."

Daniel clawed at the floor, gouging deep scars in the sand. He snapped at the air with his fangs, agitated. I wondered if it was really Daniel still inside or whether the transformation had driven him mad the way it did to Eva at first. I considered that he might bound to us and rip out our throats purely on impulse.

But he didn't.

Instead, he let out another howl, this one angry and defiant. With a vicious growl at Kaeden, Daniel turned and ran to the gate. He stopped just short of the opening and looked back, waiting for us.

"I think that's a yes," Eva said, smiling.

I grinned and nodded to Will, T-Rex, and Xavier. "Are you three up for it?"

"Am I up for it?" Will said. "When haven't I ever been up for anything? Yeah, I'm in."

T-Rex nodded. "Of course."

Xavier patted his backpack. "I still have a few tricks up my sleeve I need to field test."

I looked at Eva, and she scowled at me for even pretending to ask the question. I turned back to Kaeden.

"I'd like to say it's been a pleasure, but it really hasn't," I said. I glanced up at the gallery of werewolves surrounding us. "My friends and I will gather the Jerusalem Stones and stop Ren Lucre," I shouted. "And when that happens, things will change between men and monsters. The werewolves will need a great leader, a more just leader, a leader with honor who can lead them when this new age begins. I hope the next time we meet, you have taken matters into your own hands and chosen the leader you deserve."

The gallery broke into agitated murmurs. Small knots of werewolves pointed at Kaeden, shaking their heads.

"How dare you?" Kaeden spat.

I turned and walked away from him. The others followed my lead.

"Don't turn your back on me," he screamed. "I'm a Creach Lord. I am in command here."

"Good luck with that," I said, waving a hand at the gallery. "Seems like you might have some trouble keeping your title now that the Boros is dead."

As we entered the tunnel leading outside, the snarls erupted in a wall of noise behind us. The other werewolves jumped into the arena toward Kaeden. I shut the door behind us, closing off that chapter of our quest.

"Where to next, boss?" Will asked.

I looked at the eager faces around me, bruised and smudged with dirt. All of my friends had small cuts except Eva, who had already healed. Will leaned on T-Rex to take weight off an injured ankle. They were tired, starving, and injured, but they all wanted to know which Creach Lord was next.

There was no group I'd rather have if I had to face impossible odds and nearly certain death. Still, this next lord filled me with awful dread. I didn't know where we were supposed to find him, but something told me it wasn't going to be anywhere someone could find on a map.

"Back to the farm in Spain," I said. "We need to

rest up and heal before this next one. It's going to be unlike anything we've done before." I paused, but from the looks on their faces, I think they knew what I was going to say. "I hate to say it, but I think we need to go after the Lord of the Demons next."

Silence filled a few long seconds as each of us imagined what the Creach commanding legions of demons must look like. A loud rumble broke the silence.

T-Rex held his stomach, embarrassed.

"Yeah, do you think we could grab lunch first though? I'm starving," he said.

We all laughed, breaking the tension in the air. Then we followed Daniel, still in his werewolf form, out of the keep and back into the forest. We were ready to face the next Creach Lord, ready to face terrible monsters, and ready to do our duty. But first, we were more than ready for lunch.

A Last Note

As I warned you from the beginning, the act of reading this book makes you part of the monster hunter world. The Creach in your area have already sensed that you have this book, so you must be alert at all times.

I've set up a website to keep you posted on what's happening and to help teach you how to fight: WWW.JACKTEMPLAR.COM.

The password for the secret area is MONSTER.

See you there. But watch out...there are monsters everywhere!

Do Your Duty, Come What May!

Jack Templar

From the Author

Thank you for joining me in the world of Jack Templar and the Creach monsters. It's been my honor to get to know Jack and help him get the word out about the dangers that lurk in the shadows of our world.

If you enjoyed the book, I would appreciate a review on any of the numerous online sites where readers gather, particularly Amazon.com. If you are a young hunter, make sure to get your parent's permission first. This helps bring attention to the book and alert others who could benefit from having their eyes opened to the reality of the monster threat.

I look forward to sharing Book 5 with you...*Jack Templar and the Lord Of The Lesser Creach*.

Do your duty, come what may!

Jeff Gunhus

About the Author

Jeff Gunhus is the author of the Middle Grade/YA series The Templar Chronicles. The first book, *Jack Templar Monster Hunter,* was written in an effort to get his reluctant reader eleven-year old son excited about reading. It worked and a new series was born. His book *Reaching Your Reluctant Reader* has helped hundreds of parents create avid readers. As a father of five, he leads an active lifestyle with his wife Nicole in Maryland by trying to constantly keep up with their kids. Jeff also writes bestselling thrillers and horror novels for adults, reaching the top 100 on Amazon. In rare moments of quiet, he can be found in the back of the City Dock Cafe in Annapolis working on his next novel...always on the lookout of Creach monsters that might be out to get him! Come say hello at...

www.JeffGunhus.com

42394177R00135

Made in the USA
Lexington, KY
19 June 2015